THE GOLD COAST ALCHEMIST

Part 1

By
GERALD APPAU-BONSU

All rights reserved.
Copyright © 2022 Gerald Appau-Bonsu

No part of this publication may be reproduced, stored in a retrieval system, or transmitted in any form or by any means—electronic, photocopying, recording, or otherwise—without prior written permission, except in the case of brief excerpts in critical reviews and articles. For permission requests, contact the author at www.thegoldcoastalchemist.com.

ISBN: 9798847252515

Book Layout & eBook Conversion by manuscript2ebook.com

Table of Contents

Dedication v
Acknowledgements vii
Chapter 1 1
Chapter 2 9
Chapter 3 15
Chapter 4 21
Chapter 5 25
Chapter 6 29
Chapter 7 33
Chapter 8 37
Chapter 9 45
Chapter 10 53
Chapter 11 59
Chapter 12 67
Chapter 13 73
Chapter 14 81

Chapter 15 87
Chapter 16 91
Chapter 17 95
Chapter 18 101
Chapter 19 107
Chapter 20 111
Chapter 21 115
Chapter 22 121
Chapter 23 127

Dedication

This book is dedicated to all the people who passed away due to violence. Nobody deserves to lose their life at the hands of somebody else. No human on this earth, regardless of what they have been through or done. When I was 17 years old, my cousin was brutally murdered outside of his home. His death ended up changing the trajectories of many people's lives. It is incredible how one death can have such a ripple effect. Within the madness however is a lot of personal growth. Pressure indeed makes diamonds. The Gold Coast Alchemist trilogy whilst fictional, is based on very true scenarios I have witnessed or experienced. My only mission for this story, is to provide a raw, unfiltered perception of some of the untold stories people go through. Rest in Peace Nana Darko-Frimpong and all those who have passed away.

Acknowledgements

"I would like to thank firstly my childhood English teachers who are initially responsible for my love of reading and writing stories. They are influential in me getting to this point. I would also like to thank my editor Bettye Underwood, who helped me become a better writer. She took a manuscript that I believed was finished and showed me how unfinished it was. She did so with grace, patience and understanding. I am grateful for her help. Finally, thank you for every reader and supporter who has picked up this book, and is willing to join me on this journey. I promise to become a better writer and continue to write stories that are impactful."

Chapter 1

The sun began beating down on the dusty roads of Kumasi, and the rooster's screech indicated another morning in the busy Ghanaian city. The loud, desperate wails of shop owners could be heard as a different day began, whilst the staggering heat forced Emmanuel to wake up and begin his day. Emmanuel Mensah was a muscular man, standing six feet, three inches tall with a thick, curly black beard stretching from underneath one ear to the other. His eyebrows were equally as thick and joined in the middle.

Annoyed at the distant yelling, he climbed out of bed and made his way to the living room. Emmanuel lived in a small bungalow within the main city. The house was a simple structure, with one bathroom, one bedroom, a living room/kitchen combined. Here he stayed and worked as a carpenter, with his wife Sarah and their five-month-old son, Kwame.

"Ah, where are the bananas I bought yesterday?" Emmanuel said as he looked in the kitchen cupboards and on the shelves. "Sarah are you awake?" he yelled. He could hear her yawning next door, which was one of the many stages Sarah went through when waking up.

He went to the bedroom, where he found the love of his life, lying naked with her eyes half-open. Sarah was a short, curvaceous woman, with big, light brown eyes. Her lips were full, and she had a large, untidy Afro, which complemented her face well. She glanced toward her husband, standing at the door staring at her in awe.

"Is this the first time you have seen me?" Sarah giggled, with a smile that revealed her dimples.

"Today, I will pray to the heavens and thank my God for blessing me with one of His angels," Emmanuel said. "It is only by God's grace that I have this beauty to remind me that everything is OK. I must thank Him. But we will be late if you don't get out of bed!"

"We won't be late! Give me an hour to bathe and bathe Kwame, and we can go. Also, the bananas are in the drawer under the sink," Sarah replied.

Emmanuel humbly nodded and returned to the living room to have breakfast. Today was Sunday, a day of worship when many Christian families went to the local church and thanked the Lord for His blessings, and also to plead with God for better living conditions. Church provided Emmanuel with the hope that one day, with faith, he and his family could live a better life.

Emmanuel had grown up in poverty, working on his father's farm to survive. When his father died five years ago, neighbours took his father's land and refused to accept Emmanuel as a labourer on the farm. After that tragedy, he had to learn how to make money elsewhere to survive. After being homeless for months, he had met a carpenter named Kojo, who taught Emmanuel everything he knew about carpentry. Kojo took Emmanuel in and gave him a job within his carpentry business. In those years, Emmanuel had become an established and respected carpenter with his own house and family. He always thought back to the charity and kindness Kojo had given

Chapter 1

him, felt it was the work of God, and had praised God every day since.

"Kwame is ready and so am I, Emmanuel!" Sarah declared from the front door.

"Let's go." Emmanuel said.

The three of them headed out toward the church, a half hour's walk. It was a small building at the top of a hill, all white with a large red cross on the face of it. Inside, a long red carpet led to the altar, with twenty wooden pews on either side. At the altar stood a wooden podium with microphone. Beside the podium was a large bronze basin that shone majestically as the sunlight bounced of its surface, demanding recognition so that when people entered the church they would bask in its excellence.

Emmanuel and his family reached the church before morning mass began. Sarah exchanged cheerful hellos and pleasant small talk with her fellow churchgoers.

"Baby Kwame is growing so fast! He is adorable!" said Abena, the church choir leader.

"Abena *medasi paa!*" replied Sarah, "He will grow to be a big boy, just like his father!"

After pleasantries had been exchanged, the congregation entered the church and took seats. The service began with the choir singing a hymn. The congregation sang along with the choir in harmony, clapping hands joyfully and dancing. After the first hymn ended, the pastor entered and stood in front of the altar. The pastor was a short, obese man with a bald head and grey moustache. Sweat rolled down his bald head as he glanced around the room, his eyes piercing through everyone who had come to worship.

Emmanuel leaned close to Sarah and whispered, "It looks like Pastor James has put on weight last week. I don't understand how he can be so fat when there is hardly any food in Kumasi."

In response, Sarah giggled and slapped his leg, then placed an index finger over her lips, implying that he should be quiet.

"*Akwaaba,* my fellow brothers and sisters!" the pastor enthusiastically greeted. "Today, I have a very special sermon for you. Today, my faith in the Almighty has been solidified. Today, my faith in Jesus Christ has been confirmed. Today, my faith in the Almighty Father has been justified! Last night, I had a dream, a dream in which an angel appeared to me and said 'James, you have been preaching the word of the Lord to those who need to receive it, and the Lord is proud. More people will hear about what you have to say, and they will come to you to receive the word of the Lord.' When I woke up, I knew that God had sent me here to speak to you the way I am speaking now. However, my place of practice and worship, *our* church, is too small. We need to build a bigger church to make space for those who will soon be coming, as proclaimed to me by the angel of God."

The entire congregation went into an uproar, amazed at what Pastor James was telling them. Some were shouting, "The Lord is wonderful!" and others cried out, "God is Good!" Emmanuel and Sarah looked at each other, the eye contact between them revealing the scepticism they both felt. Neither needed to say a word, but it was obvious that they did not truly believe what the pastor was saying.

Chapter 1

Pastor James continued speaking. "To fulfil the wishes of God, who sent His messenger to me, I will need the church to help me. I would like all of you to put twice as much money into the offering as you would have done before I told you this story. God is watching all of your donations, to see if you have faith that your contributions will go to the greater good. Step up and place your offering into the holy basin. God is good!"

Immediately after the speech, the choir started playing drums, tambourines and singing songs of praise. Simultaneously, the church members danced and sang while walking down the aisle to place money into the bronze basin. Some people spoke in tongues, others lifted their hands toward the sky while praying and giving thanks. Sarah remained seated, trying to comfort Kwame, who was crying heavily due to the noise level of singing and instruments. Emmanuel also remained seated. He had a timid nature and would rather pray with private thoughts, although he enjoyed observing the enthusiasm and joy of the others present.

Pastor James looked straight at the two of them, clearly noticing that they were not participating in the festivities. He left his spot at the front of the aisle, came over to them and asked what was wrong.

"Nothing is wrong, Father!" Emmanuel replied. "God is good!"

"Aren't you and your wife going to contribute toward the offering?" the pastor asked.

"Unfortunately, I cannot. The little money I have is being used just for survival. I thank God for giving me even the little I have; it is just barely enough to feed my family and me."

He noticed an immediate change in the pastor's aura, along with his facial expression. Pastor James' previously cheerful and noble demeanour was now one of scorn and disgust. His eyes began to squint and now looked beady, and his large nose clinched as if he had smelt something horrid, like a child who had been denied use of his favourite toy.

"You have been coming to this church for years, and not once have I seen you put anything in the basin at all. Even the smallest offering will be recognised in the face of God. But no offer at all can be seen as a sign of disrespect to the most high." Pastor James declared. His abrupt, cold, and forceful tone made Sarah wince in fear.

"I'm sorry, Father, but as my husband said, if we give away our money, we will starve," Sarah replied, her voice shaking.

"Well, you will either pay now or on judgment day." The Pastor gave them an evil scowl before returning to the front of the church.

"I'm going outside," Sarah said to Emmanuel. "I think Kwame is ill. He hasn't stopped crying and he feels warm. I'll see you after the mass is over."

"Ok." Emmanuel said as he squeezed Kwame's pinky. He could tell the pastor had upset his wife. After an hour, the service ended. Emmanuel waited for everyone else to leave the church, wanting to confront Pastor James for what he said.

"Pastor James, that was an amazing sermon," Emmanuel began.

"Thank you, Emmanuel. Today is a good day! Look at all this money!" The pastor pointed to the bronze basin filled to the brim with Ghanaian cedis.

Chapter 1

The sight of all that money made Emmanuel lick his lips and swallow his saliva. He had never seen so much money in his life. He squared his shoulders and spoke his piece. "Pastor, I don't think you were right to pressure us about not giving an offering. Look at all the money others have offered the church. Would it really matter if we gave you what little we have?"

Once again, the pastor's aura changed along with his facial expression. He first glanced around the church to see if anyone remained, then removed his glasses and wiped his sweating face with a handkerchief. "Yes, it would have mattered, and it still matters. You have been coming to this church for over two years now, and not once have you paid what you owe. Everybody who comes to worship the Lord in this church must pay into the offering. You owe me at least five hundred cedis by now."

Emmanuel's heart skipped a beat. Pastor James was being serious, there was no smile on his face, just a demonic frown. Emmanuel began hyperventilating, as the shock of the moment was overwhelming. He did not have five hundred cedis and would not get five hundred cedis for a long time.

Without replying, he turned and started to walk out of the church. Before he reached the door the pastor said, "I know where you live. And I will be coming for my money tonight. My friends will pick it up for me." Pastor James laughed, the evil cackle echoed throughout the empty chapel as Emmanuel left the building.

Chapter 2

Sarah immediately began cooking lunch upon their return home. Meanwhile, Emmanuel gave his full attention to his son, putting on silly faces and playing games. Kwame, obviously feeling better, giggled with excitement, and Emmanuel gazed lovingly at his sweet, toothless smile. But Emmanuel's mind was focused on what the Pastor had told him about sending his friends here to collect. It sounded like a threat…but would he really send people to collect money? Uncertain as to whether or not to be concerned, Emmanuel decided not to tell Sarah what the pastor had said. The still atmosphere created an eerie tension within him, and he got up and locked all the doors as a precaution.

Sarah looked at him curiously. "Why are you locking the doors? Nobody ever comes here."

"Better safe than sorry," he muttered. "I'm going to put Kwame to sleep and go work on some things in the workshop."

After placing Kwame in his wooden cot and covering him with cotton blankets, Emmanuel went to the rear of his house, where he kept his carpentry tools and apparatus. Emmanuel began labouring on a block of wood with a hammer and chisel as the big golden sun set in the distance. He figured that doing some work would take his mind off the pastor's threat. An hour passed, and the sky became pitch black. Emmanuel stopped hitting the wood and wiped his sweaty brow with his hairy forearm. He wondered why Sarah had not called him to come and eat dinner. *The food should definitely be ready in the next ten minutes.*

Suddenly, a high-pitched scream broke the silence of the night, followed by the painful howling of a baby. Filled with adrenaline, Emmanuel grabbed his hammer and a nearby machete and ran into the house. As soon as he opened the back door, he leaped into the corridor looking in all directions. He felt the blow to the back of his head, and promptly fell to his knees. The screaming continued, and he realized it was coming from Sarah. She was in agony.

His hand went to the back of his head where he felt a thick liquid oozing from beneath his bushy hair.

"Foolish man," growled a deep voice from the shadows, a voice Emmanuel had never heard before. The next thing Emmanuel knew, his arms were being tied behind his back. *Am I being robbed?* In his heart he knew this was the work of his pastor.

After being securely tied up, the mystery man dragged Emmanuel into the living room. There, Emmanuel saw two masked men holding Sarah facedown to the floor. Emmanuel squawked with anger. He began rolling on the floor, shaking and writhing, trying to break out of his bondage to try and save his wife, but it was no use. Tears fell from his eyes at the sight of his beloved wife in distress. Never before had he felt so helpless, lying on the floor and watching these strange men assault his wife. The bigger man of the two gripped Sarah's neck with his right hand, while the other handheld her hands over her head. The other man sat on her thighs, trying to tear her linen skirt. Emmanuel's bottom lip trembled. "I'll kill you!!" he shouted.

Chapter 2

The skinny, smaller man sitting on top of Sarah looked Emmanuel in the eyes and smirked. "Your wife has a big ass. It's so soft!" he said before pulling down his trousers and boxer shorts and forcing himself inside her. Sarah shrieked in pain, as the man raped her. Emmanuel observed this calamity and vomited on the floor, tears rolling down his face. It sickened him to hear the man moan in pleasure as he abused his wife.

"That was amazing," the intruder said, calmly standing and pulling up his pants. "Now, where's the money you owe James? Tell us, and we won't kill you."

"We don't have any money," sobbed Emmanuel. "Please, give me one month and I will have your money, just please leave us alone."

"So, you don't have the money? That's a shame..." The man sighed. He swung his head to look at his accomplice. His malevolent grin revealed his grimy yellow teeth in the dark room. Staring at the ceiling with a demonic smile, the man chanted, "No money, no money, no money…"

Emmanuel tried to catch the attention of his petrified wife, but her eyes were closed. He wasn't even sure if she was conscious. The awkward calm was broken by the sound of Kwame crying, and all three men's eyes went to the bedroom door.

"Please, just kill me and leave my wife and son alone. They have done nothing to you. I am the one who owes Pastor James money. So I will pay with my life. In return, please leave my family alone," Emmanuel begged.

"Your life is worthless," said the man gripping Sarah's neck. "You say you have no money, but how much is her life worth to you? How much is your son worth?"

Emmanuel began experiencing cold sweats, and his heart continued pounded through his chest.

Releasing his hand from Sarah's neck, the man reached under his trouser leg and pulled out a blade. He licked the blunt edge of the gleaming knife, before gently placing it against the back of Sarah's neck.

"Who is worth more to you, my friend? Your wife, or your child? Which is it going to be?"

Emmanuel, presented with a horrific ultimatum, continued to cry in despair. How could he possibly choose? Sarah and Kwame were both parts of him, and without one, the rest of him would crumble, like ancient ruins after a heavy storm. But would it be fair to end a life that hadn't even begun? Would God forgive him for sacrificing his child to save the love of his life? Emmanuel pondered whether considering God's judgment was even necessary in this situation. After all, it was praising God that got him into this situation in the first place.

He made a difficult decision. "My son is worth more than either me or my wife. He will grow to become a king who owns many lands, just like his ancestors." Emmanuel's words were spoken softly but rang firm.

"Very well," snarled the knife-wielding man. Emmanuel cried out in anguish as the man sunk the knife slowly through the back of Sarah's neck. Blood instantly shot out of her neck, spurting into the faces of both intruders. Sarah choked and gurgled on her own blood, and then mercifully became silent and still as her life ebbed. Emmanuel's body shook with sobs as he looked at his wife's body. Kwame's crying became louder, and the mysterious man who had secured Emmanuel

Chapter 2

brought Kwame to Emmanuel and laid him down by his side before fleeing the bungalow with his accomplices. Emmanuel, his hands still tied behind his back, looked into his son's tearful eyes

"I am so sorry, son, but your mother is gone."

Chapter 3

The blood-red sun began to rise as a new morning began. Emmanuel woke up, but kept his eyes closed. He desperately wanted to believe that he had fallen asleep while working in the backyard. Emmanuel began to open his eyes slowly. His heart rate decreased when he saw Kwame's sleeping form. As his eyes opened more, he glanced at the kitchen and saw the cupboards and cabinets ripped off their hinges, placed chaotically around the kitchen counter. The large cooking pot lay on the floor, its contents now spread over the plastic tiles. Emmanuel hesitated to analyse the room, reluctant to acknowledge the horror of last night, but eventually he had to face the inevitable.

His wife lay in a puddle of blood, stiff and inanimate. Emmanuel's stomach curled, shivering with horror. He forced his wails of despair back down his throat. Kwame lay sleeping next to him, blissfully ignorant of the situation at hand. Emmanuel didn't want to disturb his son's peaceful sleep, so he forced himself to mourn his wife's murder silently.

Emmanuel worked his hands behind him to free himself from his bondage. When done, he gently placed Kwame in bed, then began digging a grave at the rear of the bungalow next to his workstation. The mental fatigue and emotional distress began to impact him physically. His triceps and back muscles ached as he furiously pierced the earth with his rusty spade. Tears continued to roll down his cheeks as he dug, dug, then dug some more. He glared at the rising sun from inside the hole. He thought back to his conversations with the pastor and became even more angry.

Emmanuel climbed out of the grave and went back to the house. He went to his bedroom and brought out two white bedsheets. Returning to the living room, he gently removed the enormous blade from Sarah's neck before wrapping her in the bedsheets, covering her whole body like a butterfly cocoon. He lifted her from the floor and carried her to her grave. Standing over it, he closed his eyes and prayed that God would receive his wife with open arms, and also that God would give him the strength to not seek revenge on the people who had so brutally violated and murdered his wife. After silently praying and reminiscing on the wonderful times he had with Sarah, he gently placed her inside the hole.

Seven days passed, and the pain and heartbreak had not gone away. Instead, Emmanuel experienced increased anxiety and a recurring dream in which an angel appeared on top of the hill on where the chapel was located. The angel, a dark brown woman with dreadlocks extending down to her feet, wore a creamy silk dress with a golden ribbon across her waist.

Bursting out of her dress were two large wings that spread so wide that they blocked the sun's light from Emmanuel's vision. In the dream, Emmanuel walked up to the angel and asked her why his wife had been taken from him. The angel told him that Sarah's murder was not the work of God, and the fact that her life was taken by a man who claimed to be a messenger of the highest made God furiously angry. After the angel spoke, the sky became dark red, and Emmanuel

Chapter 3

began falling through the air. He was still free-falling when he woke up.

Kwame cried with hunger, and Emmanuel went to prepare his son's nutrition in the kitchen. As he stirred the porridge over the stove, he kept replaying the rape of his wife in his head. Every time he thought about the night that changed his life forever, he became even more determined to seek vengeance on the pastor. Emmanuel poured the warm porridge into a plastic bowl and began to feed Kwame. As he stared into the big brown eyes of his motherless son, he concluded that it was a serious sin for the pastor to order the death of Sarah, and he must pay the consequences.

On the morning of the one-week anniversary of Sarah's death, Emmanuel cradled Kwame after he finished cleaning up his home. Emmanuel had packed away all the furniture and wooden accessories scattered throughout the house. He put Kwame down and went to the backyard, where he pulled off the dusty sheets covering his old Range Rover truck. He had not driven the vehicle in a few weeks and was sceptical if the car would even start. He placed the key into the ignition and turned it. After three tries, the engine roared, and Emmanuel grinned with delight. He quickly ran back inside and packed a bag with clothes, Kwame's milk bottle, and baby formula. He also brought the stainless-steel butcher knife that had been used to kill his wife. He put his belongings in the back of the truck, placed Kwame in the passenger seat, then got behind the wheel and drove to the nearest gas station. There he meditated for roughly five minutes. He thought about what his next move should be and whether life was even worth living. He only had two hundred cedis to his name, no wife, and a baby to look after. In the end he decided to just drive away to a new destination and start over. If he had learned anything in his life, it was that anything was possible.

Emmanuel filled his vehicle with petrol until the tank was full. Driving down the dusty road, he slowed as he approached the church. *I'll never be free until I confront Pastor James and ask why he ordered hitmen to kill my wife.*

He stopped the truck, arriving at the bottom of the hill where the Church was located. "Kwame, I won't be long," he said, leaning over his son, who already dozed in the passenger seat.

He began walking up the hill, clutching the knife that killed his wife. The closer he got to the church, the clapping and joyful singing became louder and louder. So did Emmanuel's rage and anger. He gripped the knife tighter and walked faster until he reached the chapel doors. He burst through the doors, startling everyone inside, who turned to look at him. At the front stood Pastor James with the microphone in his hand, his bald head shining in the light.

"You're late, Emmanuel," said the pastor. "Where are your wife and son?" he asked innocently, a sinful smile on his face.

"Tell the church what you have done!" screamed Emmanuel as he slowly began walking down the red carpet. Pastor James pulled a handkerchief out of his pocket and wiped sweat from his head, face, and neck. The entire congregation sat in silence; eyes fixated on the large knife in Emmanuel's hand.

"What are you talking about? You're not making any sense." Despite his claim of ignorance, the pastor sounded nervous.

Trembling with anger, Emmanuel came face to face with the pastor. Emmanuel stared into the emotionless abyss of Pastor James's eyes and tried to find honesty, truth, or humility, but found none. He thought back to the dream he was having and thought about what the angel had told him. He decided that a demon stood before him.

"Pastor, I'm only going to ask one more time. You are in God's house. You cannot lie. Tell the church what you have done. The reply you give will make the difference between life and death for you."

The pastor began to slowly pace. Then he laughed. The church members began talking amongst themselves. They knew Emmanuel was a kindred spirit and a humble man. They had never seen him show any violent tendencies. They also knew that Emmanuel and Sarah came to church every Sunday without fail. So where was Sarah now, they asked each other.

"Pastor James, what is going on?" Abena whispered.

The pastor contemplated for a few moments, then put one hand on his large belly and the other on the microphone. He moved to stand beside the bronze basin and said in a strong voice, "Last week, Emmanuel killed his wife because he thought she was a witch. Ever since then he has had post-traumatic stress. Please, let us pray for him, that the demons will leave his life."

Silence engulfed the room, as everyone looked at Emmanuel. Some got up and left the church, as if sensing something bad was about to happen that they would rather not see.

In a sudden movement, Emmanuel jumped in front of the pastor, piercing his round belly with the enormous knife. The church walls echoed with screams, wails, and gasps as Emmanuel repeatedly stabbed the pastor in front of the congregation. As the puddle of blood expanded, Emmanuel whispered to his victim, "My wife is waiting beside God in the court of judgment. You will now have to face what you did." He quickly dropped the knife and ran out of the church. No one tried to intervene. He then re-joined his son in the truck and sped off into the distance.

Chapter 4

Emmanuel drove down the highway, the wind blowing through his hair and his lungs. As he breathed in and out, he felt refreshed, relaxed, and renewed, as if killing the pastor had set the stage for him to make a fresh start with Kwame. But because killing anybody, let alone a pastor, was a crime punishable by death. Emmanuel knew he had to go far away, so he headed for the neighbouring country of Cote d'Ivoire. He knew it would take him approximately eight hours to reach the border.

As he sped down the motorway, Emmanuel looked at his son. He promised himself that Kwame would never experience the struggles he had known. He vowed to make providing for his son his number one priority.

Emmanuel pulled up on the side of the highway and bought two roasted plantains from a shop stall.

"Ete-sen!" said the stall owner, "Where are you off to! It's a beautiful day today!!"

"Me and my son are going to start a new life in the Ivory Coast," replied Emmanuel. "There is nothing for me in Ghana anymore. I have no land, no wife, and no job. Life couldn't get any worse."

"No, you are wrong! Life is good!" said the stall owner, "The sun comes up every day and provides us with energy to survive for another day. I only make enough money to last me for today. But tomorrow, I will make the same as I did today, and so on. But I still go home, kiss my wife, and laugh with my children! I am free, and I am happy."

"Yes, well I have no wife." Emmanuel responded bitterly, "But thank you for the plantain."

After a whole day of constant driving, Emmanuel and his son finally reached the Cote D'Ivoire border. As he reached the authority booth, he saw two border control officers. Both men were dark in complexion and dressed in military attire. They each grasped their rifles and wore stern, serious expressions along with ammunition belts.

One of the officers approached Emmanuel's truck. The Sergeant Major insignia on the right shoulder of his uniform indicated he was the senior of the two officers. He was a tall elderly man with a long grey beard.

"Passport, please," said the Sergeant Major. Emmanuel handed over his identification to the Sergeant. Kwame, who had been sleeping off and on during the long ride, had just awakened. As if sensing the officer's hostility, he began to cry.

"Tell your child to shut up; he is annoying me!" barked the other border control officer, a short, obese man. Emmanuel began to cradle Kwame in an effort to calm him but was unsuccessful.

"Why does your son cry so much? Is he hungry?" the Sergeant Major asked as he checked Emmanuel's appearance against the picture on the passport he had provided.

Chapter 4

"Yes, my son is just hungry, sir," Emmanuel replied. "Once we cross, I will get him something to eat."

The Sergeant Major stared into Emmanuel's eyes, as if he were trying to uncover the truth behind them. A veteran on the job, he had been protecting the border for twenty years after retiring from the army. He knew how to read people's body language; he could feel a person's energy and determine if they had something to hide. This man, Emmanuel, was setting off alarms. He remained calm, almost passive, and although he had answered all questions honestly and had been respectful, the Sergeant Major could tell something was wrong. He'd seen a mixture of emotions in Emmanuel's eyes: rage, pain, and sadness.

"My son," said the Sergeant Major, "where is the boy's mother? It is not often that we see such young babies crossing the border without their mothers."

Emmanuel swallowed. The shouting and busy chatter in the background, or the constant revving of engines by impatient motorists caught in the immigration queue suddenly became quiet, and silence engulfed the air.

"My wife passed away, I cannot stay here without her," he explained. "We are leaving Ghana to start a new life. That is the truth."

The Sergeant Major stroked his beard as he continued to study Emmanuel, contemplating the answer he'd just given.

"I could see great pain in your soul, and you have now given the reason. My prayers are with you, young man. Life is hard, but all hardships are temporary, just like our life on this earth. I wish you all the best in your travels. You may proceed."

He handed Emmanuel back his passport and the barriers opened, freeing him from the pressure and scrutiny he had just escaped. His heart began beating faster the minute he drove past the border. Sweat began to form on his palms and forehead. He had committed murder, and only now did it begin to sink in that he was now a wanted man, yet he had just successfully crossed one of the strictest borders in all of Africa. He looked over at his son and began to cry, contemplating the tough road ahead of him.

As soon as Emmanuel made his way onto the motorway heading to Bondoukou, he encountered the blinding blue lights of police cars. The lights shone so brightly in the dark that Emmanuel was unable to see the spikes that had been laid out to trap him. He took the bait, driving straight into the spikes and bursting all four tires. Emmanuel's hand reached out to brace Kwame as the truck screeched to a halt in front of a blockade of armed police officers. Above Kwame's cries, Emmanuel heard the commanding officer orders, his voice amplified by a megaphone.

"Come out of the vehicle with your hands up. You are under arrest. Come out of the vehicle with your hands up, or we will shoot you. You are under arrest for double homicide."

Chapter 5

Shell shocked by everything happening around him, Emmanuel was paralysed with fear. He stretched his hands so high in the air that had he reached any farther he would have dislocated both his shoulder joints. Emmanuel's fearful reaction wasn't in response to the commanding officer's orders or the bright lights around him, but to the automatic rifles pointed at him and his son. Emmanuel turned around to look at his son, agitating a nearby policeman by doing so. As Emmanuel caught Kwame's gaze and tried to give him a reassuring smile, the policeman standing opposite him fired two bullets near Emmanuel's feet. He began to shake. He began to analyse his situation, questioning the integrity of the police officers who had just captured him. After all, he never could have imagined that Pastor James was a man of such foul morality.

"Don't move! I will kill you just as easily as you killed your victims if you move another muscle!" shouted one of the police officers.

Once more Kwame began to cry.

Emmanuel experienced the same helpless feeling he had during Sarah's assault and murder. *Could they actually kill me in front of Kwame? Or worse, could they kill Kwame in front of me?* In addition to his fear, Emmanuel also felt regret and relief, but also confusion. "Double homicide?" he pondered, his lips barely moving.

"Who are they saying I have murdered? What are you talking about? I don't know anything about this," Emmanuel shouted, shaking his head for emphasis. "Please don't hurt my son. He is in the car, and he's just a baby."

The officer who had shot at Emmanuel began to slowly approach where he stood, keeping the rifle aimed at his head the whole time. Another officer followed close behind and searched Emmanuel thoroughly, before signalling for several other officers to join him. Emmanuel was ordered onto the ground by three large and bulky S.W.A.T team soldiers. He was handcuffed and left with his face in the dirt. As he lay on the ground face down, the police officer who had initiated the arrest flipped him onto his back and placed his boot on Emmanuel's chest. The repulsive, coarse sound of a snort followed, and then the officer spat on Emmanuel's face.

"You piece of shit," the officer growled. "You are going to rot in hell for the lives you have taken. You will pay for the lives you have ruined."

Emmanuel used his mouth to try to blow away the mucus on his face. Although he was furious at how the officers had treated him so far, he remained calm, still paralysed with fear as he watched the officers removing Kwame from his truck. As he was dragged into the back of the police wagon, he began to cry as he saw his son taken away by strangers in an unmarked vehicle. Where were they taking him? Would he ever get to see his son again? Tears flowed from Emmanuel's eyes as both vehicles sped off in opposite directions. He closed his eyes and began to pray. Although his faith had been rocked by the recent tragic events in his life, it was still second nature for him to appeal to a higher power for refuge and answers.

Chapter 5

His lips moved in silent prayer. "God, why have you forsaken me? What did I do to deserve this? All my life I have followed the Bible's teachings. I have lived a good life and try to be a good man. Why? What did I do?" He raised his shoulder to wipe away his tears.

It felt like they had been driving for hours before Emmanuel finally succumbed to his fatigue. He was awakened when one of the officers slapped him in the face. He shrank back, then realised they had stopped, apparently having reached their destination. As Emmanuel was removed from the back of the police wagon, he looked around at his surroundings. He saw a large, ancient-looking Moorish castle with several outposts surrounding it. The fortified structure intimidated Emmanuel even more than the armed guards stationed in front of it.

"Welcome home, inmate," whispered the commanding officer into Emmanuel's ear.

"He still needs to stand trial. He isn't one of ours just yet," stated the receiving officer at the prison gate. She was the first female officer Emmanuel had seen since his apprehension on the highway. She looked so much like his wife, that he thought his mind was playing tricks on him. She looked at his bruised face with compassion. He felt as if she were trying to empathise with him amidst the chaos. The officers who had beat him up left him in the custody of the female officer. Her soft hands provided a somewhat awkward relief momentarily as she rested them on top of his handcuffs. Emmanuel began to reminisce about his wife Sarah, and his memories of good times with her making him smile.

His euphoric nostalgia was interrupted when the officer began to tighten his handcuffs, which were already tight enough to cause bleeding during the ride to the prison. Emmanuel winced in pain.

"You're handsome, but I take no chances. Especially with murderers. Let's go!" The officer pushed him down the hallway into the prison. The hallway was like a maze, with different rooms at every turn. Emmanuel felt himself getting lost. The deeper he went inside the prison, the more lost he felt.

After several minutes of walking, he was thrown into a small cell that had nothing inside it besides a bed and a small hole in the ground, with a bucket beside it. The walls were stained with blood and faeces. A metallic screech could be heard as the doors locked behind Emmanuel, sealing him into the tomb. Trapped in complete darkness, Emmanuel began losing his perception and cognitive functioning. He lay on the dirty concrete floor, trying to distinguish if the voices he heard were coming from one of the other prisoners, or if they were a manifestation of his loneliness and cognitive deprivation. He began to cry as he contemplated the future, licking his own tears in an attempt to satisfy his thirst for water, having been deprived of hydration for several hours. Emmanuel closed his eyes and dreamt of the time so recently when he was hugging and kissing his wife and child. His body was screaming for rest, but it was impossible for him to sleep, not knowing what had happened to Kwame. His insomnia kept him awake for several days.

Chapter 6

As the rising sun began to force its way through the tiny cracks and natural windows of Emmanuel's cell, the prison could be heard waking up. One inmate screamed *"Bonjour les detenus, baise les colonisateurs!"* That meant nothing to Emmanuel, who didn't speak any French. He was truly in foreign territory.

The same officer who had locked Emmanuel in the cell several days ago, had returned.

"How was your sleep?" she asked him.

"What sleep?" he replied.

She chuckled before asking him to turn around and put his hands through the slot in the prison door. She then placed him in the handcuffs, reopening the cuts that had attempted to heal over the last few days. She opened the cell door and escorted Emmanuel to a building opposite the cell block where he was being held. To his eyes, the courthouse and its courtyard were a magnificent creation. After spending days in the isolation of his cell without much light, being taken to the courthouse within the Moorish fortification was a shock to his senses. He was able to appreciate everything within the square that preceded the courthouse doors. Statues and sculptures stood throughout the gardens. The sweet scents from the various plants in the garden almost intoxicated Emmanuel as he was led past them. Assuming he didn't have much time left to live, he tried to take in as much as possible. When he and his escort reached the courthouse, the steps leading to the entrance gleamed brightly as the sun reflected off the marble. The banisters at both sides were made of gold and shone even brighter in the light than the elegant marble steps. Emmanuel wished he could turn and look behind him at the beautiful gardens but was forced to go inside and face his destiny. The ancient courthouse for centuries had been the destination of many legendary criminal justice cases throughout the ages. It had become the place where all serious trials would take place in the Ivory Coast.

As the guards opened the doors to the courtroom where Emmanuel's fate would be decided, he saw a spherical theatre-like setup filled with people who appeared to be lawmen, scholars, and religious figures. The room, which had been buzzing with conversation and proclamations, fell silent when Emmanuel entered. All that could be heard were his footsteps as he walked forward and the rattle of the chains that bound him. As he continued to walk to where he had been instructed, light murmuring resumed as the courtroom occupants began to talk amongst themselves.

Emmanuel proceeded to stand in a booth labelled, "Accused".

As he entered the booth, he was locked inside it and was then requested to put his handcuffed hands through a slot in the middle of the booth's door. Once unshackled, Emmanuel turned and faced the crowd.

The loud bang of a gavel silenced the crowd, and the court session began. The gavel was held by an elderly woman with long, silver dreadlocks. Her gold-coloured silk robes and jewellery indicated that

Chapter 6

she was of high status, obviously a judge. The room remained hushed as she continued to read through the notes in front of her. Emmanuel watched on in suspense.

"Emmanuel," the judge finally said. "My name is Karimah Ngwewe. You have been brought to my court today because you are accused of murdering a pastor named James Nkrumah, in his own church, in front of his congregation, all of whom have written testimonials of what they witnessed on that day. Not only are you charged with the pastor's murder, but you are also accused of the murder of your wife Sarah Mensah, the mother of your only child."

Emmanuel stared at Judge Ngwewe as the charges against him were read. He reminisced over his actions, and how vindicated he felt by stabbing Pastor James to death. He was content with those actions but being accused of murdering Sarah gave him an indescribable anguish, like a disease eating him from the inside. He would never harm Sarah, let alone kill her. She had been his only light and reason for living before Kwame was born, and a part of her lived on in the son they had created together.

"I did not kill my wife," Emmanuel said to the judge when he was given permission to speak. The spectators began murmuring amongst themselves. "I loved my wife, and she loved me. We lived a simple but perfect life. About a week ago, Pastor James sent men to my house demanding payment of an offering. They raped and tortured her. I couldn't help her. They caught me by surprise. In the end, they asked me to choose which person they would kill, my son or my wife. I wish they had just killed me instead." Emmanuel began weeping quietly.

Judge Ngwewe studied the young man in the booth as he wept. She believed that he loved his wife very much, proclaiming his innocence to the court before his legal representative even gave his opening statement. But now was not the time to muddy her judgment with personal opinions.

The courtroom began to buzz with reaction to Emmanuel's heartfelt statement. Although the courthouse was within an old Moorish structure and decorated with various African artworks, the court was structured very similar to its colonial powers, the French. Both the prosecution and the defence barristers wore scarlet gowns and wigs, keeping with tradition.

Representing Emmanuel was a young man named Tobias Richards. Tobias was a young law school graduate who had volunteered his time, as no other barrister wanted to take Emmanuel's case. Tobias was a young caramel-skinned man with a curly-haired afro. He also had freckles across his face and on the back of his neck. Underneath his scarlet gown was a slick black-and-grey suit. His shoes were shined perfectly, so much so that light reflected off them.

Tobias slapped the side of the booth where Emmanuel stood and whispered, "Be quiet and let me do my job. My job is to save your life, and I cannot do that with you opening your mouth. So please, say no more!"

Tobias then turned and went to the podium and proceeded to give the judge and jurors his opening speech.

Chapter 7

"It is a privilege to be presenting this case to you, Your Honour. You are famous for your fairness and consideration for ethical matters when it comes to human rights violations. Now, I first want to state that what happened to the two decedents is an absolute tragedy. We are here today to talk about the truth behind these awful events. The defendant has stated that although he will admit to killing Pastor James, he did so in self-defence after the pastor had sent mercenaries to his house after the defendant was unable to provide a contribution to his church, according to the defendant. The defendant is claiming that these are the people murdered his wife. Your Honour, we ask that you remove the second murder charge against Emmanuel Mensah, as he is innocent of this crime, and spare him the death penalty in reward for his honesty in this matter. Thank You, Judge."

Judge Ngwewe remained silent after hearing Tobias' opening statement, offering acknowledgement by nodding her head slightly, before turning to the prosecutors. The prosecution team consisted of three lawyers sent by the Ghanaian government, two men and one woman. The leading prosecutor was a middle-aged man named Kwabena Frimpong. Although Kwabena was almost sixty years of age, he appeared to be in excellent health and possessed a muscular physique. He was bald, with a thick white beard. Originating from the Ashanti tribe and standing at six feet, five inches, Kwabena had a distinctive presence in the courtroom.

He stood and approached the podium. "Your Honour, we are here today in the name of justice," he began. "I very much agree with the young gentleman representing the accused when he says these murders were a tragedy. A horrific series of events that should never have transpired. After a very thorough investigation, we can say that James Nkrumah was a man who dedicated his life to God and his church. He has never previously been accused of anything negative by anyone. To be stabbed to death and accused of extortion by the defendant is abhorrent. James Nkrumah is not here today to dispute Emmanuel Mensah's claims. Perhaps it would have been the pastor today standing in that booth, instead of the accused. Those of us who believe in God, believe that regardless of whether the pastor did these things he is accused of, revenge in the form of murder is the worst thing anyone can do. Regarding the brutal sodomy, mutilation, and ultimate murder of Sarah Mensah, we have both physical and circumstantial evidence that points to Mr. Mensah as the person who committed these horrid acts. Besides this evidence, we also have an eyewitness who states he saw Mr. Mensah strike his wife before going into hiding for his own safety. We ask today that Emmanuel Mensah be sentenced to death for the murders of James Nkrumah and Sarah Mensah. Thank you, Your Honour."

As the lead prosecutor returned to his table and spoke softly with his team, the spectators began whispering amongst themselves again. During this intermission, Emmanuel contemplated what the lead prosecutor had just said. Who was this witness they were talking about? The only other witnesses he knew of were the ones who had killed Sarah. Surely it couldn't be them?

Chapter 7

Emmanuel also thought about the morality of his actions. Even before he killed the pastor, he knew it was wrong to kill other living things. He knew that was against the God he believed in. He thought back on the dream he had, in which the angel had come to him. As he looked at the judge in front of him, it occurred to him that she looked exactly like the angel in his dream. They had the same facial features and skin tone. What did it mean? The angel had told him that the pastor was not of God and was in fact a pagan. Emmanuel considered that if he was sentenced to death without hopes of personal redemption, that perhaps he would meet the archangel who came to him in his dream at the pearly gates. Maybe she could plead his case to the gatekeeper. He chuckled, his thoughts drowning out the chaos in the courtroom.

The bang of the gavel gradually made the crowd become quiet.

"The time has come for the prosecution to present their witness in regard to the charge of murder in the first degree of Sarah Mensah, aged twenty-seven," proclaimed the judge.

"Your Honour," said Kwabena, "for his own safety, our witness has asked to be interviewed in a secret location, because he does not wish to reveal his face to the jury."

"What is the credibility of this witness, Your Honour?" Tobias asked. "It seems unfair that an unknown witness can identify and provide testimony about my client's actions without verification. This is unheard of!"

The judge hesitated, appearing to be considering the matter. "I can understand a witness's reluctance to appear in court when the case involves this degree of violence. If the witness did indeed see this horrific act with his own eyes, then I can understand his apprehension.

However, I agree with the defence that whilst the witness does not have to appear in this courtroom, complete anonymity undermines the credibility of the witness. The witness will appear in person." stated Judge Ngwewe. "We're adjourned until tomorrow morning, at which time we will hear from your witness, Mr. Frimpong."

Once again, the spectators in the courtroom murmured amongst themselves about this latest development in the case.

The next morning, the court session began, and the witness was brought into the court room to begin giving his testimony. After everyone had been seated, the court's head assistant announced the start of the witness presentation.

Chapter 8

Emmanuel watched on eagerly as his accuser was brought forth. The witness was a large dark-skinned man, with light brown eyes and a scar that ran down one side of his face. He was bald with a thick moustache that nearly concealed his top lip. He smiled, revealing jagged yellow teeth. This huge beast-like figure smiling in the manor he was, terrified those in the courtroom as they observed him.

Suddenly, Emmanuel closed his eyes and began screaming uncontrollably. Everyone in the courtroom turned to look at him in the booth as it began to rock from his leaning back and forth, nearly falling over with him inside.

Judge Ngwewe slammed her gavel down in an attempt to regain order. "Order in the court!" she demanded. "What is wrong with the defendant? Why is he screaming? Mr Richards, control your client!"

Tobias looked at Emmanuel and then back at the Judge and shrugged his shoulders. "I have no idea, your Honour." Said Tobias.

Emmanuel's head limply dropped forward. He had screamed himself hoarse. Seeing the witness's face had triggered a flashback, and in an instant, he now clearly remembered the events of the night his wife was murdered.

He remembered being awakened by the sound of Sarah's screams. He remembered being ambushed from behind when he went to investigate. He remembered how Sarah was punched in the face and stabbed. He remembered Sarah, his darling wife, being sexually abused, raped, and ultimately killed. And he remembered who had done that to her. The prosecution's witness, who was ready to testify against him, was none other than the man who had murdered his wife. Of that Emmanuel was positively certain. He stared at the killer as the killer stared down the courtroom, smiling at his audience.

"The defendant should be aware that he shall be found in contempt of court if there are any more outbursts," Judge Ngwewe admonished. "There will be an opportunity to rebut the witness's testimony. You are expected to conduct yourself appropriately at all times. Do you understand?"

"Yes, Your Honour," Emmanuel replied.

Emmanuel's heart began beating a mile a minute. Up until now, he had been in almost a zombie-like state as his fate unfolded in front of him. He looked at Tobias and said "This is the man who killed my wife. What is going on here?!"

Tobias stared at the witness, and then back at Emmanuel. Tobias wasn't an experienced lawyer, he'd always had a way with people. He knew how to distinguish whether a person was being honest. He decided that Emmanuel was telling the truth and that this monstrous-looking man that stilled the courtroom, may indeed be a violent murderer.

Tobias turned and stood once again on the podium, to question the witness.

CHAPTER 8

Tobias turned and looked at Emmanuel one last time. The young lawyer saw truth in Emmanuel's eyes. Tobias then cleared his throat, inhaled deeply, and then exhaled intensely.

"Good afternoon, Witness X. My name is Mr Tobias Richards. Would it be appropriate for me to ask to call you by your first name?" Tobias inquired,

"Objection, Your Honour!" bellowed the lead prosecutor Frimpong. "This line of questioning is inappropriate and undermines the anonymity of our witness!"

Before the judge could rule on the prosecutor's objection, the witness calmly replied, "My name is Kwaku Bonsam."

There was an eerie silence as the witness revealed his name. His voice sounded incredibly deep as it vibrated around the room. He slurred his words as he grumbled, and his chest rattled as he spoke. His physical presence intimidated those in the courtroom, but his accompanying voice and demeanour terrified everybody present. None other however was more horrified than Emmanuel, who was once again taken back to that fateful night in which his wife was murdered. He would never forget the voice that whispered twisted and demeaning words into Sarah's ears as she was raped and murdered, and he would never forget the base in the laugh that followed. Tobias turned to check on Emmanuel's state, and Emmanuel was not doing well at all as he stood shaking in the booth.

"Mr Bonsam, could you please tell the court your whereabouts at around nine o'clock in the evening, Friday, the twenty-eighth of January, nineteen ninety-nine?" Tobias queried.

"I was walking on my way to buy some plantains from the local salesman near to Ash-Town when I heard an argument coming from a house. A man was yelling and cursing at a woman, who was crying and occasionally yelling back at him," Kwame said. I walked up to the house and looked in the window. the man was trying to have sex with the woman, but apparently, she did not want to. The man slapped her and pinned her down."

Before he could continue, Emmanuel screamed out "STOP! PLEASE, STOP. ADMIT WHAT YOU DID TO MY WIFE! ADMIT IT!" The judge slammed her gavel down, and then again as the courtroom became chaotic once more.

"Order in the court!" demanded Judge Ngwewe, "That will be the last warning, the very last warning for the defendant. We understand the emotional connection within this case, but outbursts of any kind will result in the defendant being returned to his cell and charged with being in contempt of court. Now, the witness may continue".

Kwaku smiled from ear to ear, like a demented clown who couldn't contain his excitement as he continued to tell his story.

"The man beat up the woman and forced his way inside her. After he was done, he stabbed her multiple times and slit her throat. I would have tried to save her, but I am a coward, and I had no weapon. I'm disappointed to say that I ran away. I saw the appeal for information a week later and I had to come forward. Of course, the cash reward was an incentive, but I couldn't bear the weight of what I had seen. It feels good to get it off my chest."

The spectators seemed awestruck by the witness's account. With boiling rage, Emmanuel noted the relish with which the witness told his story. Couldn't everyone see through his empty claims about feeling relieved? He turned to Tobias and whispered, "This man definitely is the one who murdered my wife, and he wasn't alone that night. He

Chapter 8

had at least one accomplice who restrained me whilst this monster carried out the attack he just described. His description is accurate, except it was him who did that to Sarah, not me."

Tobias contemplated his strategy for the upcoming line of questioning. He contemplated the best way to get the witness to confess. Tobias also contemplated how this could be the case, and the prosecution did not know about it? Whilst West African civilisation had a lot to do in order to catch up to their European counterparts, Ghanaian police did have access to DNA testing, albeit it was in its infancy. If this man had indeed committed these crimes, it shouldn't be too late to prove it. Of course, Emmanuel's DNA would also be found at the crime scene. Tobias ran his fingers through his afro as he pondered his next move.

"So, Mr. Bonsam, when you went to the police with this information, what did they do?" Tobias began.

The witness hesitated. "Can you be more specific?"

Tobias cleared his throat. "When you went to the police with this information, did they treat you as a possible suspect?"

"No."

"And you never actually entered the deceased's residence, you merely saw these events unfold through the window. Is that correct?" asked Tobias.

"That is correct, yes."

"So it's safe to say that based on the information you provided them, they immediately moved to make you a witness before verifying your story with evidence?" Tobias prompted.

"Objection, Your Honour!" cried Kwabena Frimpong. "This line of questioning undermines the investigative tactics of the detectives, and therefore undermines the credibility of our eyewitness. The defence is trying to create uncertainty amongst the jury!"

"Overruled. Answer the question, Mr. Bonsam," the judge ordered.

"What kind of guilty man hands himself over to the police without admitting a crime? I am a witness because I witnessed a crime taking place. That is all," said Kwaku.

"Thank you, Mr. Bonsam. That is all I have for you," said Tobias before turning to face Judge Ngwewe. "Your Honour, my client has informed me that his traumatic outburst earlier came from a jolt in his memory upon seeing Mr. Bonsam on the screen. He says that Kwaku Bonsam is actually the person who murdered his wife, Sarah. He doesn't understand how the killer has been able to become the prosecution's star witness, and I must add that neither do I. It is my client's right to be able to accuse someone else who could have committed the crime. The witness has stated that he stood outside a window and at no time did he enter the residence. A brutal rape and murder of this calibre will leave behind huge amounts of DNA, which I state will be able to place the witness inside the home and on the victim's body."

The prosecution team began talking amongst themselves in a panic, in between their internal deliberations, they would look at the Judge, Emmanuel, before Kwabena stepped up to the podium.

"Your honour, the only DNA samples law enforcement officers were able to collect on scene were the defendants and the deceased. There were no other DNA profiles on the scene." Said Kwabena.

Chapter 8

Emmanuel began shaking with anger and disappointment as the reality of the events unfolded before him. He could see the witness laughing and smiling. Emmanuel felt at that point, that all hope is lost.

"Fair enough." Said the Judge, "Does the prosecution have any questions they would like to ask the witness before we move on?"

"No your honour," Said Kwabena, "I believe the defence has done my job for me. Nothing further your honour".

Kwabena's demeanour as he laughed his way back to the prosecution's bench, paired with the witnesses' clear misguided intentions meant something was wrong to both Emmanuel and his attorney. Tobias looked at Emmanuel in shock, as if he had just been revealed to the true reality. Tobias knew that it is impossible for Emmanuel and Sarah's DNA only to be in the house. What about their child? What about the second attacker according to Emmanuel? Things just weren't adding up. Tobias began to panic as the jury was escorted out to start deliberations.

Chapter 9

Emmanuel had been through one of the most soul-destroying, absolutely devastating last few days. The past few days had seen Emmanuel's emotional state mimic a rollercoaster, with all its twists and turns. The chaos had taken its toll on the Ghanaian carpenter. After the trial had ended, Emmanuel slumped into his temporary cage, with his head down. Tobias could see that Emmanuel's will to fight for justice had been eradicated by the crooked system. Emmanuel had entered the courtroom with the spirit of a strong-willed runaway slave determined to earn his freedom. The events that followed eroded that determination and conviction. Emmanuel understood now that the world does not operate on truth and honesty, and that justice is a mythical concept given only to those with the privilege of wealth, power, or privilege.

Sentencing day had arrived. Once everybody had entered the courtroom, the attendees in the courtroom began their final round of whispers as Emmanuel began taking deep breaths. He closed his eyes whilst inhaling and exhaling. His muscles began to relax, and his heart began beating at a normal pace again. Whilst he was convinced, he would be convicted for a crime he didn't commit, he did indeed kill the pastor. Emmanuel had come to peace with this already. Emmanuel reckoned any outcome would only bring him closer to being reunited with the love of his life. For about sixty seconds, Emmanuel was at peace. His piece of mind however was shattered by the uncertain outcome for the fate of his son. Emmanuel began reversing his relaxation process, he began hyperventilating as he made his way onto his feet. He looked at Tobias and called him over. Tobias hadn't taken his eyes off Emmanuel this whole time and had witnessed his internal struggle and metamorphosis.

"What's wrong Emmanuel?" Enquired Tobias.

"I do not know the whereabouts of my son. He was snatched away from me when I was arrested, they wouldn't tell me where they were taking him. I don't know if he is even alive. After the way events have unfolded, it is not unreasonable to question the integrity of those who took my son? I have come to peace with my fate Tobias. But what of Kwame? What will happen to my child who is innocent of all of this?" Asked Emmanuel.

Before Tobias could reply, Judge Ngwewe had returned to her bench ready to commence with the final stages of the trial. All stood at attention as the Judge took her seat, before sitting themselves.

"It seems the jury after deliberating has finally reached a verdict." Said the Judge. "Please bring them in."

Emmanuel's heart began pounding heavily, trying to escape its rib cage prison to no avail. For this was judgement day. The foreman of the group of Jurors stood up and began to read the verdict.

"On count one of the murder of James Nkrumah in the first degree, we the jury find the defendant guilty. On count two of the murder of Sarah Mensah in the first degree, we find the defendant guilty. On count three of reckless driving and endangering the public, we find the defendant guilty." Bellowed the foreman.

CHAPTER 9

Emmanuel tried to gain some kind of eye contact with the jurors, but they would not glance in his direction. Some looked ashamed and troubled with the verdict. Others looked fulfilled and confident. All of them however did not want to acknowledge Emmanuel soon after ending his life more or less. Emmanuel looked at Tobias, reminding him to enquire about his son.

"Not yet." Mouthed Tobias as he told Emmanuel to calm down by raising his hand up and down in the air.

The judge looked through the case notes in front of her one last time as the courtroom fell still awaiting the Judge's response.

"When this case was presented to me, the gruesome nature of this crime connected with me on an emotional level. Both victims, in this case, seemed to be upstanding citizens of the community that they resided. One being a preacher and member of a church congregation. The other, a young beautiful mother who leaves behind a beautiful young baby boy. One fact has been confirmed and not disputed by the defendant. This is the murder of James Nkrumah. Emmanuel, whilst I understand how one can be pushed to the edge of morality and sanity by others, I cannot accept that anything that happened to you would call for such savagery. You stabbed a person repeatedly, ignoring not only the immorality in such an act but also the horrified screams and wails of spectators. Earlier in the court, you stated that you did not kill your wife and that the murder of your wife is what drove you to murder the pastor. The truth in this remains to be discovered. However, if indeed what you are saying is true and your wife was murdered by men ordered by the pastor, acting in the name of vengeance and killing the pastor was not the right thing to do. No one man has the right to be a judge, jury, and executioner. No matter the reason. It is for this reason that I find you guilty of crimes you will have to answer for. I sentence you to life in prison for the crimes you have committed. I hope you can understand the gravity of the crimes you have committed, and also find peace before facing God."

Judge Ngwewe slammed her gavel twice. The room was silent for a second, besides the sound of spectators exiting the courtroom. Tobias looked at Emmanuel who was crying, with his head held high. Emmanuel looked at the Judge as she began to exit the courtroom. His fists were clenched in a ball, and he was shaking profusely.

"WHERE IS MY SON?!" Screamed Emmanuel. "WHERE IS MY SON!"

Emmanuel's cry shattered the silence, and those who had begun to leave stopped in their tracks. The Judge looked up at Emmanuel in shock. Emmanuel repeated his question and began chanting this.

"WHERE IS MY SON?! WHERE IS MY SON? WHERE IS MY SON?...." Shouted Emmanuel.

The Judge called one of the police captains forward to the bench.

"Where is his son?" She asked the police officer. The police officer shrugged his shoulders before whispering a message in the Judge's ear.

They deliberated between themselves for about five minutes before the prison officer instructed his fellow officers to remove Emmanuel from the booth and return him to his cell. The Judge looked at Emmanuel one last time before exiting the courtroom.

As Judge Ngwewe exited the courtroom, Emmanuel began screaming louder.

"NO! Don't ignore me! Where is my son? Please just tell me where he is. What is going to happen to Kwame?!"

CHAPTER 9

The Judge kept walking and ignored Emmanuel's questions. As the judge exited the courtroom, four officers proceeded to try and restrain Emmanuel. Immediately after the door to the booth was opened, Emmanuel proceeded to kick one of the officers in the chest. The kick immediately knocked down the officer, who fell landing on his back. The other officers were startled after this. Although Emmanuel was restrained by handcuffs, it seemed Emmanuel was still very dangerous. One of the officers lunged at Emmanuel in an attempt to capture him. Emmanuel kicked the officer in the chest but was soon tackled by another officer who had used his fellow officer as a decoy to get to Emmanuel. The officer charged Emmanuel to the ground before properly restraining him. Once restrained, Emmanuel was dragged back through the forecourt garden, back to his cell. On his way back to the cell, Emmanuel tried to take in the aromas and scenery one last time, but he was unable to savour these moments like he did when he was coming into the courthouse. The guards who had apprehended him made sure he was swiftly taken back the way he came. As he was led down the hallway in which his cell resided, Emmanuel could hear the other prisoners taunting him.

"Bienvenue à la maison!" Said one prisoner. "Get used to the smell!" Said another. Both released a maddening chuckle after their taunts. Emmanuel was thrown into the cell. Before the letter box in his cell could be closed, Emmanuel lunged and put his arm through the slot.

"Move your arm or we will break it." Said the commanding officer.

"Please." Sobbed Emmanuel, "I won't cause you any trouble if you can tell me where my son is? Is he safe? Is he alive? Just tell me he is ok, or I will not survive until tomorrow."

The guard who had threatened to break Emmanuel's arm immediately proceeded to make true of his threat by closing the slot with Emmanuel's arm still through the slot. Emmanuel winced in pain before withdrawing his arm through the slot. The slot was closed, and the guards walked away. Emmanuel listened to their footsteps get quieter and quieter, as he looked through the crack in his cell. He began to pray about his son as he attempted to drown out the wails and cries around him. He understood that this was his home now and that he would have to get used to it. Emmanuel wasn't worried about the solitude or the sordid conditions in which he would remain. He only cared about his son, and what was to happen to him. It would be these thoughts, along with the thoughts of Sarah and the Pastor that would torment him for years to come.

Illustrated by Volodymyra Sokur

CHAPTER 9

Kwame's Fate: Prologue

After his father was taken by the police in Ivory Coast, Kwame was taken back to Ghana where he was handed over to a child custody agency. There Kwame stayed for about a few weeks while authorities waited for the fate of his father, Emmanuel. After Emmanuel was sentenced to life in prison, and it became apparent that there was nobody available to look after baby Kwame, the authorities began adoption proceedings. Kwame was visited by many potential foster families within two months. Some offered to take Kwame to their upper-class life in Nigeria, South Africa, Spain, and even Abu Dhabi. The family that ended up taking Kwame home, however, was a middle-class British couple of Ghanaian descent. Their names were Julia and Frank Amponsah.

Julia and Frank Amponsah were a young British couple who lived in Camberwell, which is situated in south London. Julia Amponsah had been a professor at King's College University before choosing to quit and look after her mother after she was diagnosed with terminal cancer. After her mother passed, she decided to dedicate her life to volunteering, focusing her efforts on cancer research. Frank Amponsah was a tradesman who knew many trades and ran his own company which specialized in plumbing and electrical services. The Amponsah family had been trying to have a child for almost a decade before deciding to adopt instead. After hearing Kwame's tragic story, Julia and Frank felt compelled to provide Kwame refuge in their loving home and provide him with all the love his parents would have given him.

After completing their adoption of baby Kwame, the Amponsah family brought him to their home in London. Here he was raised as a normal child, oblivious to the circumstances that had brought him to the United Kingdom.

Chapter 10

The rush and chaos of the concrete jungle in which Kwame resided always played a key part in getting him out of bed in the morning. His mother yelling his name helped, but the roar of engines from passing cars and buses together with the sound of motorists' horns were just some of the noises that filled the air as London woke up.

"Wake up, Kwame! You're going to be late!" shouted Julia from downstairs.

"Please, Mum, can you call Mr. Power and tell him I can't come in today because I'm sick?" Kwame suggested.

Kwame tried to get back to sleep but heard his mother stomping up the stairs. *No, leave me alone! Let me sleep…*

Julia burst into Kwame's room. "If you're really sick, then you're not going to stay in bed all day. Get dressed, and let's go down to A&E. Of course, we'll probably be there longer than it'll take for you to get to school and back! Your choice," said Julia.

Kwame grumbled in frustration before removing his duvet and kicking his feet in the air to further express his dissatisfaction. Julia shook her head and giggled as she made her way back downstairs to finish making breakfast. As Kwame made his way to the bathroom,

Frank emerged from the master his bedroom and lightly slapped Kwame on the back.

"Have a great day, young man. Every day is a new opportunity to be the best you can be. Remember that!" Frank said.

"Yeah, yeah, I know," Kwame mumbled.

After making it down the stairs, Frank took a piece of buttered toast Julia had prepared before kissing her goodbye and heading out the door on his way to work. This was how things would go almost every morning, it had become their routine. Julia prepared a filling breakfast…eggs, bacon, and pancakes, waffles, or French toast, and he rarely sat down to eat. Instead, he'd grab a muffin, a piece of toast, or a breakfast burrito and gobble it on his way to work.

"Come on Kwame, you're already late," Julia called again. "Hurry up and come eat your breakfast."

Kwame smoothed the shirt of his school uniform. He was just starting Year Eight, the second year of secondary school. His first year had been a learning experience. One of the things he'd learned was that you weren't cool if you wore the school uniform the way the school wanted. For that reason, Kwame always wore his shirt untucked. Paired with a sharp level one fade and a fresh pair of kicker boots and his Nike "Just Do It" bag, he was ready to enter Year Eight as one of the most fly teenagers in the school.

Kwame hurried downstairs to the kitchen and sat down. He quickly indulged himself in the meal his mother had prepared: pancakes topped with fresh strawberries, blueberries, and a sprinkling of powdered sugar. Julia sat next to Kwame and fixed a small plate for herself, but she beamed at him more than she ate.

Chapter 10

Kwame slowly stopped chewing his food and looked at his mother. "What is it, Mum? Why are you looking at me like that?"

"I'm just thinking of how much you've grown, Kwame. I'm so proud of who you're becoming, despite your reluctance to go to school. Knowledge is power, Kwame. Throughout your life, you might obtain material things and gain new relationships. Neither of those things will necessarily last, but no one can ever take away the knowledge you have in your head or the fire inside your heart. Keep learning and growing. Work hard in school so that you can chase your dreams without needing anybody but yourself."

Kwame finished eating, hugged his mother, and kissed her on the cheek before leaving for school. As always, he travelled to school with his closest friend and next-door neighbour, whose given name was Christopher but was known by the nickname "CJ." Kwame walked down to CJ's flat, which was a floor below his, and knocked on the door.

"CJ, hurry up, man! I don't want to end up in detention for being late again. You know Mr. Power loves to chat shit as well!" he called. After another five minutes, CJ came out and they headed for St Joseph's Secondary School, which was located in West Norwood. From their estate in Camberwell, travelling through various neighbourhoods in London was equivalent to travelling through no man's land into the enemy territory.

Kwame and CJ made their way to the bus stop down the road. When the bus came, they took their seats at the back of the upper deck.

"So, are you going to the football trials today?" CJ asked.

"Yeah, of course," Kwame replied. "But only because they're allowing us to go in fourth period. I hate maths, man. Any chance I get to skip that class, I'm gonna take it."

"Here I was, thinking you were going to football try-outs because you're one of the best strikers in our year, but instead you're only going to pass the time? You're a wavy footballer Kwame big man ting. You should be trying to get yourself scouted by one of the major football academies."

Kwame just shrugged and looked out the window.

Kwame, CJ, and the other students on the bus got off at Crown Point. Crown Point signified the crossroads where their secondary school was located. At Crown Point, buses could be taken in any direction: north to Camberwell and Brixton, east to Crystal Palace and Sydenham, south to South Norwood and Croydon, and west to Streatham. Therefore, Crown Point was a stop-off for students from various schools. For Kwame and the other students at St. Joseph's—an all-boys Catholic school—it represented a chance to meet and socialise with female students.

When Kwame got off the bus, he went straight into the bakery that faced the bus stop. It was called Tracey's, after its owner. Tracey was renowned for making some of the best cookies around.

"Yo, CJ, wait for me, please. I'm just going into Tracey's for a sec!" Kwame said over his shoulder as he jogged to the bakery. As he entered, he joined the queue of students waiting to place their orders. He noticed his latest love interest, a girl called Natasha, a few spots ahead of him. Natasha went to Virgo Fidelis High School, an all-girl's school east of Crown Point. Natasha was a beautiful girl with a caramel complexion and green eyes. She had braided her hair and decorated

Chapter 10

it with pink shoelaces. Her plump lips glistened with sparkling lip gloss, and her teeth were pearly white. Kwame smiled as he watched her giggle amongst her friends. One of Natasha's friends whispered in her ear, which prompted her to turn around and look at Kwame. His heartbeat sped up as he smiled and waved at her. She turned around and continued laughing with her friends before getting her order and leaving the shop. Kwame collected his order soon after and tried to find her, but she had disappeared, likely proceeding on her journey to school, so Kwame rejoined CJ and made his way through the school gates which was just down the road from the shop.

Chapter 11

As his form teacher, Mr. Power, called out names for the register, Kwame yawned and stretched as he contemplated the long day ahead of him.

He rested his head on his desk as he tried to drown out the chaos of energy and noise colliding around him. He closed his eyes and pictured the moment he had shared with Natasha just a few minutes earlier. He loved seeing her smile and contemplated how he could make it happen again. Descending into his fantasy, he did not hear his form tutor calling his name.

"Kwame? Kwame? Kwame Amponsah!" Mr. Power's voice got louder with each repeat.

Kwame suddenly became aware and snapped out of his daze. "Yes, sir!" he answered, his classmates laughing at his slow response.

"Kwame is buzzing, fam!" said one of the students, his remark meeting with more laughter.

After the register had been taken and Mr. Power had gone through the day's agenda, the form class was dismissed. Kwame had a long day ahead of him. His first two periods were English and Religious studies, followed by Maths which he hated. The lessons had become routine to him, and the morning lessons seemed to fly by.

Every student looked forward to lunchtime. The hour break not only offered students the opportunity to eat lunch, but also to participate in the many sports activities within the school grounds such as football, pat-ball, and four-square, among other activities. Kwame usually spent his time selling the food and drink he had bought at Tracey's Bakery before school. Some favourite snacks weren't available in the school cafeteria. Students who wanted these goods could purchase them on the school's "black market," in which Kwame was a willing participant and top salesman. He specialised in selling what he called "meal deals" which included a drink, a packet of crisps, and a chocolate bar. He sold the "meal deal" for only one pound. The popular package always sold out within the first twenty minutes. After selling his stock, Kwame would make his way to a hidden part of the playground, where students could be found playing "pound-up", a gambling game that involved throwing a pound coin toward a wall. The person whose coin landed closest to the wall was first in line to collect all the coins and bet heads or tails before flicking all coins in the air. They could then collect all the coins that landed on the side they'd called. The person whose coin landed the next closest to the wall repeated the process. Almost every student wanted to partake in the pound-up game at lunchtime, for one could multiply their finances rapidly. A student who came to school with two pounds could leave with ten or even twenty more. However, only those of significant status or popularity were allowed to take part. "Neeks" or "Nerds" risked being robbed before the game even began.

Kwame joined five other students to commence the next round of "pound-up." Kwame's coin landed closest to the wall; however, the person who came in second claimed he was first. His given name was Clarence, but he went by the nickname "Tiny Eyez".

CHAPTER 11

"Nah, what are you doing, bro? Can't you see man's up?" Tiny Eyez said to Kwame.

"What the fuck are you talking about?" Kwame replied. "Are you blind? Can you not see I'm up?"

Tiny Eyez replied not with words but with a punch to Kwame's face. Kwame was initially stunned by the sucker punch, but regained his composure immediately, launching a flurry of punches and combinations that would have made Mike Tyson proud. A three-punch combination knocked Tiny Eyez's two front teeth out of his mouth, along with a clot of blood. Tiny Eyez then attempted to hold Kwame to stop the attack he had initiated. As Tiny Eyez grabbed Kwame and pushed him up against the wall with his head in Kwame's chest, Kwame glanced around and saw his fellow students laughing. All of them had their phones out and were recording the altercation.

"Oh shit, Mr. Power is coming!" one of the students warned. Everyone promptly scattered away from the gambler's den.

Mr. Power came around the corner to see a bloodied Kwame, who by now had captured Tiny Eyez in a headlock who was in severely worse shape.

"Hey! Get off of him!" Mr. Power demanded as he charged toward the pair and proceeded to separate them.

"He started it!" said Kwame.

"Nah, I ended it, pussy!" Tiny Eyez replied.

"You can tell it to the headmaster!" Mr. Power calmly replied.

"Nah, please, sir. I have football trials next period!" Kwame pleaded.

"You should have thought of that before you started fighting like a bunch of wild animals!" Mr. Power snapped.

Kwame and Tiny Eyez, having each been treated by the school nurse, sat opposite each other outside of the headmaster's office. The headmaster's assistant watched nervously as the beaten and bruised teenagers stared each other down. Possibly feeling another outbreak of violence, she stood, but at that moment the headmaster abruptly opened his door. Both boys snapped out of their stare-down and sat at the ready.

Mr. Connolly, the headmaster, was a tall man at six feet, two inches. He wore his blond hair in a bowl cut and a thick, bushy moustache. Always well dressed, today he wore a grey suit along with his famous two large rings and gold watch. Mr. Connolly smelled of a blend of cigarettes and aftershave and had a habit of constantly wiping the sweat from his forehead with his handkerchief. The headmaster looked at both Kwame and Tiny Eyez, then pointed at Kwame and ordered, "In, *now!*"

Swallowing hard, Kwame stood and swiftly entered the office, sitting in one of the chairs opposite Mr. Connolly's desk. Mr. Connolly walked around to his desk and sat. He stared at Kwame for a long moment, analysing Kwame's rapidly swelling left eye and the cut on his lip. He then sighed heavily.

"What are we going to do with you, Kwame?" he said. "You can't keep doing this. This is the third fight you've been in this year. You've also left school early and left the school grounds during break times. Do you want to be here, Kwame?"

Kwame, eyes still on the floor, shrugged.

Chapter 11

"I don't understand it. You have so much potential, Kwame," Mr. Connolly continued. "The next few years of your life are crucial to your development as a man. You can be anything you want to be in life, but in order to get there, you need to focus on being the best person you can possibly be. Dedicate these next few years to becoming knowledgeable and ready for the world."

Kwame continued looking at the floor.

"Look at me," Mr. Connolly demanded. Kwame looked up and met the headmaster's gaze, his eyes brimming with tears. He got up from behind his desk and gave Kwame a fatherly hug. The pain in Kwame's eyes had overwhelmed him. Mr. Connolly knew Kwame was an adopted child and sensed he felt somewhat different because of it.

"I'm sending you to isolation for the rest of the day," He told Kwame. "What you did was wrong, and you need to spend time reflecting on your actions. I was initially going to give you some lines to write, but we will leave that for now. Clarence's parents have been called to pick him up. He needs to see a dentist right away. If you and Clarence thought you'd be going to football trials after this, you can forget about it."

Kwame left the headmaster's office as Tiny Eyez was ushered inside and headed to the isolation room, which he knew very well. It was a small room directly above the school chapel. It contained a single chair and desk, along with a camera in the top right-hand corner of the room that was aimed at the desk. All natural light was blocked out by built-in shutters locked in position. When Mr. Connolly (at the time a military veteran just one year into his new vocation as a teacher at the school) first proposed establishing an isolation room, opinions of parents, educational staff, and the regulatory body were divided.

Some compared it to a mild form of solitary confinement. Others said the sensory deprivation it caused was a human rights violation. In the end, Mr. Connolly was able to present his case that placing the most irritable and disruptive students in periods of isolation was highly effective in changing behaviour, offering them time to reflect on the actions that landed them there. Repeat offenders were usually instructed to write lines in their notebooks to reinforce the lessons that needed to be learned. Kwame spent two hours alone inside the isolation room. As the headmaster decided not to make him write the usual eight pages of lines (the same phrase written over and over again), Kwame was left only with his thoughts. He thought about the weird moment when Mr. Connolly hugged him. The unusual act confused Kwame, but it also made him feel quite good for reasons he didn't quite understand. After an hour or so, all Kwame could think about was that he was missing football trials because of Tiny Eyez and a stupid gambling dispute. Growing more and more infuriated, Kwame started punching the desk.

"Stop punching the desk," ordered a voice through the intercom. Kwame recognized Mr. Connolly's voice. He must have been keeping an eye on him through the CCTV surveillance system.

After spending the entire afternoon in isolation, the day was over and Kwame re-joined his friends as they left school for home.

"Fam, football was too sick. Kwame, I'm sorry you missed it. There were a couple of scouts there from Arsenal and Crystal Palace!" CJ's voice rang with excitement.

Kwame just frowned as he took in CJ's smiling face.

Chapter 11

CJ started laughing and hugged Kwame. "Why you screwin' me, man! I'm not Tiny Eyez. Bro, go do that with them, man!" CJ chuckled.

Kwame tried to slap CJ on the back of his head but missed when CJ ducked with swift agility. CJ continued laughing as he jogged ahead. Kwame couldn't help but laugh as well as he jogged behind CJ to get on the 468 bus. Kwame and CJ went to the upper level and sat in the back. After a long and exhausting day, Kwame rested his head against the window and closed his eyes.

Several stops into their ride, CJ noticed some "centre boys" getting on the bus. Centre boys was the term for those who had been deemed too bad to attend school, so instead were assigned to a centre for troubled youths. These boys were considered the worst of the worst.

"Shit, Kwame," CJ muttered. "Those centre boys are coming up here. Maybe we should go down."

"Fuck that! I'm not scared of them. Plus, I'm just minding my business on the way home from school. I'm not in the mood for any drama."

CJ quickly gathered his belongings to move, but it was too late. Before he had slipped on his backpack, he saw three hooded males dressed in all black, almost as if that was their uniform. Black hoodies, black Nike puffer jackets, and black cargo trousers. The only thing that differed was their choice of footwear. The one that caught Kwame's eye wore black and green Nike Air Max 90's. He was the largest of the three and seemed to be the leader of the group. He was the only one of the trio who had a thick beard, and he also had a scar across his temple. His very presence put fear in the hearts of everyone who saw him.

The minute they reached the upper deck, they took it hostage. One stood in the stairway, blocking anybody who tried to go to the lower level, whilst the others proceeded to rob the passengers. They targeted schoolchildren and women.

"What you got for me?" they said as they shook the schoolchildren's blazers. The jingling of coins revealed their location in the children's pockets, and the centre boys proceeded to take their money. The boys robbed everything valuable that the passengers had, from money to phones, and even their food and drinks. Then they reached the back of the bus where CJ and Kwame sat.

"What you got for me?" asked the fearsome ringleader in a deep rumbling voice.

"I don't have anything for you, big man," Kwame replied. "Why are you here sucking little kids? Why don't you go bother people your own age?"

CJ looked at Kwame in shock, and then at the centre boys in fear as he awaited their response. The leader paused for a second as he stared at Kwame with hostility in his eyes. He then cracked a smile before punching Kwame in the face. The leader then dragged Kwame into the middle of the aisle before he was joined by his friends. All three of them began to punch and kick Kwame repeatedly. They would have beat Kwame to death had it not been for the sound of sirens in the distance, which forced them to flee down the steps and off the bus. Kwame managed to weakly smile at CJ, revealing his blood-covered teeth, before losing consciousness. A tearful CJ screamed for help as the other passengers scrambled down the steps in their haste to get off the bus. The driver stopped the bus off and ran upstairs to join them. "It's okay, young man," he said soothingly to Kwame. "The ambulance is on its way."

Chapter 12

Kwame woke up to the sound of hospital equipment beeping. As he opened his eyes, he saw his mother at his bedside, and his nightstand was covered with flowers and get-well cards.

His mother rejoiced at his opening his eyes. She clapped her hands. "Thank God! My baby's awake!" She leaped out of her seat and hugged Kwame. "I am so sorry this happened to you."

Kwame screamed when his mother squeezed him too tightly. Her grip intensified his pain. His attackers had broken one of his ribs, caused severe bruising over his entire body, and caused his jawline to swell up like a basketball.

"I'm sorry, baby!" said Julia as she released her son. "Here, drink some water."

As she held the water bottle to her son's mouth, he winced in pain and then shook his head, declining the opportunity to drink more water. Julia returned to her chair. "I should let the nurse know you've woken up." She started to get up, but at that moment a nurse entered the room. "Well, look who's awake."

"I just woke up," Kwame said. "I hurt all over. Can you give me something for the pain?"

"Of course."

"I tried to give him some of my water, but it hurt him to drink," Julia said in a worried tone.

"Don't worry," the nurse assured. "Your son is on a drip, which will provide him with all the necessary nutrients he needs."

"Thank you," Julia whispered. "What is going to happen now?"

"I'm going to add some pain medication to his IV," the nurse said, "and then let the doctor know he's awake. He'll then come to examine Kwame. Excuse me, I'll be back shortly."

Thirty minutes later, after receiving pain medication, Kwame was already snoring again, Julia lovingly watching her son as he slept.

The door burst open and Frank rushed into the room. He gasped in horror at seeing his son in such a terrible state, then began hyperventilating. Frank bent over Kwame's bed, his breaths audible and ragged. Julia quickly jumped up and pressed the emergency call button on Kwame's remote. Kwame awakened, his eyes widening in terror at his father's obvious difficulty breathing. A white-smocked doctor entered the room, closely followed by the nurse.

"Sir, you're having a panic attack." The nurse guided Frank to a chair. "I want you to take slow, deep breaths."

Frank managed to nod and followed the nurse's advice. The doctor who had just walked in at this moment, watched him carefully, and when he was satisfied, he began informing the Amponsah's about Kwame's condition.

"I want to begin by saying your son is lucky to be alive. He's suffered a broken jaw, a broken rib, a broken arm, and internal

CHAPTER 12

bleeding. Fortunately, we were able to stop the bleeding during surgery. He's going to have to wear a brace around his jaw also for the next few weeks."

After Kwame's condition stabilized, he was discharged and began his road to recovery from his Camberwell home. Three weeks out from the attack, Kwame still couldn't talk properly, and his arm was still casted, although it wasn't hurting quite as much to cough because his rib was healing. Julia had taken a leave of absence from work to look after her son. Kwame needed help with dressing and bathing. After another two weeks, Kwame was doing much better and decided he was ready to get some exercise.

"Mum, I'm just going to the park. I won't be long. I just want to stretch my legs and get some fresh air," He said after successfully struggling to tie his shoelaces with his nearly healed arm.

"Don't be too long, and make sure you don't wander off. Be sure to keep your phone on. You're always putting your phone on silent and missing my calls!" Julia said with a smile. "I'll be right here making your dinner."

"Thanks, Mum." Kwame opened the door with his good hand. He made his way to the park just outside his block of flats. He sat on a swing and began taking deep breaths. He kept thinking about the attack. He thought about every second and every action made. `As he winced in pain, he thought about his decision to verbally confront the centre boys when everybody else had kept quiet and complied with the robbery. He contemplated the fact his pride had led to his being beaten.

"I'm not a prick." Kwame whispered to himself as he sat on the swing.

He looked up and saw a group of youths walking through the park. As most of them wore hooded jackets that drooped over their faces, Kwame's heart began racing. Could these be the same boys who'd beaten him? Or Tiny Eyez, coming to settle the score following their lunchtime fight?

As the group got closer, Kwame determined that he had never seen any of them before. They walked toward Kwame. They were dressed differently, but they all sported the same black bandana. The tallest of the bunch also looked a little older than the others, a light-skinned young man with dreadlocks that fell to his shoulders. His mouth held a long cone-shaped marijuana cigarette, which he took huge drags from periodically. He held a leash, with what looked like a red-nosed pit bull on the other end. The dog seemed agitated. He approached Kwame as the others stood back and observed.

"Yo cuz, what's good?" greeted the man holding the dog.

Kwame nodded his head cautiously as he awaited the next question.

"My name is Darker. The small chipmunk-looking yout on the BMX is Rex. The girl next to him is his sister Renee, but she's known as Younger Queenpin. The twins are Jack and Jax, but they go by Gader and Bauser. And this cutie" —he nodded toward the dog— "is my baby girl, Lion. Even though she's a dog, she's my favourite girl, you understand?" Darker bent to stroke Lion's belly.

"One of my young G's told me about what happened to you on the bus. That's fucked up."

Kwame wondered if the gang had been waiting for him to make an appearance in the park.

Chapter 12

"I know them men that jumped you," Darker said. "They're proper wet youts, bro. They're from Peckham. They roll with them Peckham boys. I heard it was Tiny Stack and Younger Shocks and them man there. But hear what though, you see you, you've got heart, my bro, and I fuck with it. I came all the way here to tell you that I salute how you handled yourself." Darker held out his fist.

Kwame's caution gave way. He extended his fist to meet Darker's, connecting the spud.

"Yes, my yout!" said Darker before laughing and turning to look at his peers. "You look like you're in pain, my Y.G. You know a couple pulls of this good food will help you know. Have you smoked weed before?" Darker asked Kwame.

Kwame had never smoked anything in his life, but he didn't want to look like a nerd in front of Darker, so he lied and nodded his head. Darker handed Kwame the spliff. Kwame took it and inhaled. He took such a huge hit that even Darker widened his eyes with surprise. Kwame removed the spliff and began coughing. Darker and his friends laughed.

"You're actually a Spartan man. We need you on our team," Darker said through his laughter. "What happened to you won't happen anymore if you start rolling with us man. The men that jumped you are cowards, bro. They prey on people who can't protect themselves. On top of that, you live on Crawford Estate, bro. Certain men can't even come 'round these sides. More time them man would say we can't go 'round them sides, feel me?" Darker smiled. "I want you to become my younger. You're worthy enough to be. But if you do, then you're gonna have to work, just like the rest of us. The work is hard, but the pay is good. You're gonna be able to get all the new creps and get all the gyal!" He reached into his pocket and pulled out a huge stack of £50 notes. "This is what I've made today, and it's not even three PM, " he said before putting it back in his pocket. "So, what you sayin'? You rolling with us man?" he asked Kwame.

Kwame contemplated the offer as he tried to figure out what the catch was. He wondered how he would fare without this affiliation, especially after everything that had happened to him. Kwame didn't have any brothers or cousins. He felt like he had no one to call upon if he did need help.

After a few moments he made up his mind. "Yeah, I'm rollin' with you man."

Chapter 13

After Kwame's injuries completely healed, he felt like a new man as he prepared to go back to school. He felt rejuvenated and ready for anything. Not only did he feel physically stronger, he felt mentally stronger. Standing up to the attackers on the bus had put a fire in Kwame's belly. He had stood up to the bullies, and although beaten badly, he had survived. Not only that, he'd just been initiated into the gang on his block. They were already notorious for numerous illegal activities, along with their longstanding rivalry with other gangs. Their main rivals were a small gang stationed in Peckham, who only a few months ago killed two of Darker's associates at a Burger King drive-through restaurant. They executed a drive-by shooting, firing a MAC-10 and a Desert Eagle into the packed restaurant, hitting their targets but also three civilians. The tragic murders ramped up the already intensive gang war between the Peckham and the Brixton based gangs, and it had been like the Wild West ever since.

Kwame thought about that and all the other implications of his gang affiliation as he put on his school uniform. Buttoning his shirt, he muttered to himself,

"Fuck it. Better to fuck with the gang than to get fucked with every day. I ain't a prick."

"Kwame, breakfast is ready!" his mother shouted from downstairs.

"Coming, Mum!" Kwame picked up his hairbrush and went over his hair before making his way to the kitchen to eat breakfast.

"You don't want to miss the early bus," his mother said. "It's the late bus that always has those rowdy boys who cause trouble."

Her words barely registered in Kwame's brain. His mind was preoccupied contemplating the possibilities of the day.

A knock sounded on the door. Julia went to get it as Kwame continued eating.

CJ stood on the other side of the door. "Good morning, Mrs. Amponsah! Is Kwame ready yet?"

"I'm ready, man!" Kwame called out, his words mumbled because of his last bite of breakfast. He grabbed his backpack, putting it on as he rushed to the door. He gave Julia a quick kiss on the cheek. "Bye Mum! Love you!"

Kwame and CJ began walking to the bus stop. CJ noticed Kwame was quieter than usual.

"Look bro, I'm sorry for what happened. I tried to tell you. We should have gone downstairs when the centre boys came on the bus." Said CJ

"Listen CJ, I'm not a dickhead. I'll never let someone treat me like one either. If they killed me, I would have died with my dignity. I won't lose it for anybody." Said Kwame.

Kwame gave CJ a deadly glare, before continuing his walk to the bus stop. CJ felt chills down his spine as Kwame talked to him. He knew with absolute certainty, that Kwame really believed in what he was saying, and that he would indeed die before laying down his beliefs. His admiration for Kwame grew tenfold within that moment. CJ admired Kwame's conviction and bravery. Beyond that, Kwame had saved his life on that bus. CJ felt indebted to him.

"I hear you bro." Chuckled CJ

"You know your name's ringing out now," CJ said with admiration. "People are talking about how you fucked up Tiny Eyez and stepped up to the centre boys."

Kwame suppressed a smile. He wondered if Natasha would be interested in him now. He felt welled up with confidence and promised himself that he'd make Natasha his girlfriend before the half term holidays. He felt untouchable, now that he was Younger Darker and had the backing of his new friends.

Kwame and CJ hopped on the bus to Crown Point. When they arrived and got off the bus, Kwame heard a female screaming his name, like he was a rock star. To his delight, it was Natasha.

"Kwaaaameeee!" Natasha screamed as she ran toward Kwame with her arms wide open. When she reached him she gave him a big hug. "I've been so worried about you! How could you be so reckless? Don't you know you have people who care about you?"

"Like who?" Kwame replied, looking into Natasha's eyes.

She blushed and released Kwame, taking a step back, "Don't be silly!" With that, Natasha turned and she walked back to her friends.

Kwame stood watching her, smiling, knowing she was going to turn back to him.

She did just that. "I'm glad you're OK." She said as her and her friends disappeared inside the bakery.

Kwame walked into his class feeling great. Students he had never spoken to before were shaking his hand and nodding at him. Was this what respect felt like? He was only receiving a small amount, but it was intoxicating.

At lunchtime, Kwame made his way to his usual spot—the gambler's den in the back of the school playground. As he walked across the football field where many year seven pupils were playing football, the freshmen immediately halted their movements when they saw him go by.

"Oh, shit!" shouted one of the youngsters. "That's Darker's new younger!"

"Ain't that the guy who smacked up Tiny Eyez?" another student asked, loudly enough for Kwame to hear.

Kwame did his utmost to resist the urge to grin from ear to ear as he walked across the field. Instead, he opted for a stern screw face, spreading the look across the young students in an effort to strike terror into their hearts. Only after Kwame had crossed the field did the students resume their game.

As Kwame turned the corner, he was greeted by a crowd. In fact, it seemed like the majority of the student body was waiting for him. As soon as he came into view, all chatter ceased, the school playground momentarily falling silent. It was eerie, so much that it made Kwame's heart skip several beats. Everything seemed to move in slow motion as he scanned the crowd. Everyone was looking at him, then their gazes shifted to someone in the back of the crowd, but he couldn't fully

CHAPTER 13

see who it was. As the figure drew closer Kwame realized it was Tiny Eyez, and he was taking off his jacket and backpack—a classic signal of an intention to fight.

"Here we go!" screamed one of the students with excitement. If there was one thing that all students loved to witness, it was a fight. They had missed the first altercation between Kwame and Tiny Eyez, even though news of the fight later circulated throughout the school as Kwame took weeks off to recover. Not only had the fight circulated among students at his school, but it had also gone viral at other schools, too. Tiny Eyez had been waiting to face Kwame again, and the time had come for him to try and earn back his stripes. Kwame knew he could beat Tiny Eyez if he had to fight him again, and that it would give him even more stripes…but as he looked around at the crowd, who was chanting *"Fight, fight fight!"* he realised that in the end, the only people who would lose were him and Clarence. Mr. Connolly had warned him that he would be expelled if he was caught fighting again. *If I get expelled, there'll be no more hugs from Natasha in the morning. No more GCSEs. Or worse. I can't jeopardize that…*

"Listen Eyez," he began. "I don't want to fight you, man. What happened last time is a minor."

Tiny Eyez started charging forward, pushing his way through the crowd. The crowd started chanting louder, "Fight! Fight! Fight! ". Tiny Eyez ran toward Kwame like a bull seeing red. Kwame actually saw the rage in his eyes.

Kwame assumed a fighting stance as Tiny Eyez threw a jab-hook combination. As he began swinging wildly, Kwame swiftly sidestepped the incoming barrage, managing to manoeuvre behind him. He wrapped his arms around his waist, lifting him and slamming him into the ground. The sound of his body hitting the concrete echoed through the playground, instantly silencing the crowd. As Tiny Eyez lay flat on the ground, Kwame sat on his back. "I *told* you I didn't want to fight you. This is what happens when you choose to bring out the beast." he hissed.

He then got up and walked away. Behind him, he heard Tiny Eyez coughing and gasping for air. The hair on the back of Kwame's neck rose as Clarence yelled after him.

"You're dead! You're fucking dead, I swear to God! Just wait. I'm gonna get you set after school. Remember I told you!!"

In spite of the chill that ran through Kwame, he continued walking away and didn't look back.

During the entire period after lunch, Kwame's mind kept going back to Tiny Eyez's threat. He pondered whether he had really meant what he said. *Does he really mean to kill me?* Kwame could tell from the way his classmates looked at him that they'd heard about the impending showdown. Kwame considered leaving school early to avoid Tiny Eyez and his gang, but quickly decided against it. Not only would he lose his reputation if he did that, but he'd have to leave early every day from now on. If Tiny Eyez had held a grudge against him all this time, he wasn't going to let this one go…

Then he remembered what Darker had told him. This was the exact situation they would want to help with. Kwame took out his phone and sent Darker a text message, looking at the teacher every few letters to make sure he didn't get caught.

Chapter 13

T. Eyez is pissed I fucked him up, he said he's going to kill me after school. He's going to bring his mandem. I need backup!

Within two minutes Kwame received a reply:

SNM my young G. We're en route.

As he made his way to his last class before school let out, Kwame heard his classmates whispering amongst themselves and saw them looking at him. Some even held small notebooks and pens, suggesting they were running bets on the outcome of the impending battle.

Chapter 14

When the school day came to an end, Kwame looked around and saw his peers clearing their desks, packing their textbooks, notebooks, and pens into their bags. He rested his head on the desk to cope with the butterflies that had formed in his stomach. His mouth felt dry and his heart was pounding. Mr. Power approached Kwame as the last students left the classroom and came to sit at the next desk.

"What's wrong, son?" Mr. Power asked. "You're usually a right nuisance in my class, always mouthing off and being the class clown, but not today. Today, you were quiet as a mouse, and now you're sitting with your head lying on your desk when you're usually the first one out the door once the bell rings. What's going on? Don't you feel well?"

Kwame raised his head from the desk and looked at his teacher in the eyes. Kwame wanted to confess the situation in which he'd found himself, but he also didn't want to be branded a snitch. He figured that would only make the situation worse, so he stood and picked up his book bag.

"You're the safest teacher I've ever had, Mr. Power. I'll see you tomorrow," Kwame said as he left the classroom.

After joining CJ and walking out of the school, Kwame quickly realised that the crowd around them was even larger than the one during lunch break. Apparently, the word about Tiny Eyez's threat had spread, and everyone had stayed behind to watch the situation unfold. A large huddle formed behind Kwame and CJ as they walked toward the gates. When Kwame looked up the main road, he noticed that Crown Point seemed busier than usual. As he stood at the gates frozen with fear, he contemplated turning back and seeking refuge with Mr. Power before pushing that thought to the back of his mind. He closed his eyes and silently mustered up the strength and courage to face what was to come, then took a deep breath and nodded his head before clicking his knuckles and moving forward.

Crown Point was the usual meeting point for drama and regular secondary school traffic, and as Kwame approached he started scanning the large crowd for Tiny Eyez. He spotted him in the company of two other males who appeared much older than fellow secondary school students. One of the men wore a red Avirex jacket, with a red New Era fitted cap with black jeans, black Air Forces with red shoelaces. Half of his hair was braided, the other half hung free in a wild afro. The other man with T. Eyez was short and stocky, wearing nothing but a vest, tracksuit bottoms, and house slippers. Both men had several young students lined up against a wall. They were robbing each student of their money, phones, and other valuables as each student stood frozen in fear.

"Oh, shit, man! That's Eyez from Blood Gang!" CJ's voice was filled with fear.

"Which one?" Kwame enquired.

Chapter 14

"The one dressed in red, you donut! Oh, shit, man!" CJ repeated. "I always thought Tiny Eyez was lying about being his younger. He shanked up my cousin last year. He's crazy, man!"

Kwame froze again when Tiny Eyez spotted him. He stared for a long moment, then tapped his older accomplice Eyez on the shoulder and whispered in his ear and walked in Kwame's direction. All three of them left the robbery scene and began running toward Kwame, the short and stocky one taking out a huge stainless steel kitchen knife. The knife was so clean that the light reflecting off it gave a blinding streak of light. Kwame and CJ turned and ran in the opposite direction. At that same moment, Kwame's phone began vibrating in his pocket. He knew it must be Darker, so he pulled it out as he ran.

"Darker?" Kwame said, breathless.

"Yeah, it's me, my young G. Where are you now?"

"They're chasing me!" Kwame yelled. "They're gonna kill me, man! One of them has a fat bora. I need you to come *right now!*"

"Where are you now?" Darker asked a second time, his voice annoyingly calm.

"I'm just about to go down Norbury Hill! Please come fast, they're gonna catch us!" Tears ran down Kwame's face.

"We're coming. Just stay on the phone with me," Darker said.

Kwame and CJ ran past the school and turned down the long, steep Norbury Hill. Kwame could run much faster than CJ, but he kept his speed at CJ's pace as he didn't want to leave him behind. A quick glimpse back revealed that Clarence and his friends were getting closer.

"*I told you I was gonna kill you, you fucking neek! Why are you running?*" Tiny Eyez shouted.

Kwame looked at CJ, who was slowing down. "Come on, CJ! We have to keep going, because someone's coming to help us and they'll be here any minute. Just keep going!"

Panting heavily, CJ stopped. "I'm sorry, Kwame I can't go on. You go. I'll be fine. They're not after me, anyway." CJ waved Kwame on.

Kwame reluctantly resumed running down the hill. He looked back to see if Tiny Eyez and his allies would attack CJ. Eyez and T. Eyez, both faster than their stocky companion, ran right past CJ without acknowledging him as they chased Kwame. Relieved, Kwame turned to look at where he was going.

Within seconds, he heard a terrified scream. His instinct told him the scream had come from CJ. Eyez and his younger had ignored him, but their stocky companion likely had not. Tears filled Kwame's eyes as he recalled that huge knife the man had held…but he pushed through his sobs and kept running.

He had almost reached the bottom of the hill when he heard a car speeding down the hill and the loud thumps as it hit each speed bump. The car screeched to a stop in the road beside Kwame. Inside was Darker and two other individuals, one of whom was a fair skinned black female who quickly hopped out of the vehicle. Kwame was almost taken aback by her beauty, although she was dressed in a simple tracksuit and wore no makeup. She stood in front of Kwame and raised her hand which was covered by a sock, under which Kwame recognized the shape of a gun.

Eyez and Tiny Eyez caught up to Kwame, coming to a stop just a few feet away.

CHAPTER 14

The beautiful young woman gripped the wrist holding the gun with her other arm. "I should kill you right now for stabbing little kids for no reason. Are you fucking sick in the head?" she said, her voice low and threatening.

"Are you fucking mad? Do you know who you're talking to?" Eyez demanded. "You should be at my crib waiting to suck my balls. This life ain't for peng tings like yourself." Eyez said with a sly chuckle. Tiny Eyez and the heavyset dude with the knife, who'd caught up to them, joined in.

The young woman let out a sarcastic chuckle of her own before calmly firing two shots at CJ's attacker. One of the bullets went straight through his forehead, and the other went through his neck. He fell backward, already dead. Kwame trembled in shock and fear. He looked at Darker, who sat in the front passenger seat of the car serenely smoking his spliff. Darker met Kwame's eyes and nodded his head.

Fear showed on Eyez and Tiny Eyez's faces as they looked down the barrel of the gun. The unmistakeable sound of someone urinating filled the air. Kwame saw a wet spot spreading in the front of Tiny Eyez's pants.

"I'm sorry," he cried. "I swear to God, I'm sorry, man. I didn't expect all of this to happen. Please don't kill me. Oh, God! I just want my mum!"

Eyez looked at his friend's dead body lying on the ground, then at the trembling Tiny Eyez. "Bitch," he muttered. "I ain't goin' down like that."

He lunged forward, pulling out a knife from under his jacket. He shouted, "You must think I'm some pr—"

He never got to finish the sentence. The young woman fired. The first two shots hit him in the arm and shoulder, causing him to stagger back and allowing her to aim better. The other two hit him in the chest.

"Get in the car," she ordered Kwame.

He stood there, looking at the vehicle reluctantly.

"I said, get in the fucking car!" she yelled. Kwame snapped to attention and quickly got into the backseat of the green Volkswagen Polo. The young woman stepped over Eyez's body to approach Tiny Eyez, who was visibly trembling, obviously fearing he would be next. She kissed him on the cheek and whispered in his ear, "You're only alive right now because I don't have any bullets left. If you're built for this, I'll see you again." Clarence vomited briefly onto his shoes before running away, crying.

The gunwoman ran back to the car as the sirens in the distance became louder and louder.

Illustrated by Ramone Lewis-Harris

Chapter 15

Kwame sat in the backseat of the speeding car, shell-shocked. His ears were still ringing, and the lingering smell from the gun made him want to throw up. He kept thinking about his best friend, who no doubt had been stabbed to death. Kwame began hyperventilating severely.

Darker turned around and patted Kwame's knee. "Just take a deep breath."

Kwame took three deep breaths, which served to stop his hyperventilation. Darker then offered him his spliff. "Hit this, my young G. It's the good shit, I promise you. Proper flavours. It'll relax you."

"Listen." Darker said as Kwame took a drag, "What just happened isn't your fault. If we didn't find you, them men would have deaded you off. You saw what they did to the little white kid. Even if he was your friend or not, you could tell that the kid was harmless, man. Proper fucked. But again, it's not your fault. None of it is. Do you understand?"

Kwame nodded his head, then began to cry.

The young woman who had come to his rescue, who sat beside him in the back seat, gave him a big hug. Then she wiped his tears and cupped his chin.

"Listen to me. From here on out you can't be crying around me. I'm going to allow you to do it this one time because I know you're young. But we can't have any soft niggas on our team, you understand? Weak links break the chain. Anyway, my name is Rachel! People call me Sweets, others call me crazy! It's a shame we had to meet under this mad situation."

Kwame looked at her and then at the gun she had placed in the back pocket of the seat in front of her. She was definitely a very dangerous individual, but had beauty, elegance, and an energy about her that intrigued him. She seemed incredibly calm after just killing two people.

"I just want to go home," Kwame mumbled. Darker poked his head through the space between the front seats and exchanged looks with Sweets, then signalled something Kwame didn't understand to the driver. They drove into a nearby car park and parked. The driver and Sweets both removed the top layers of their clothing, revealing different outfits underneath, and exited the vehicle. Sweets took the weapon before winking at Kwame.

Darker looked back at Kwame. "Come join me in the front."

Kwame reluctantly exited the car and sat in the driver's seat.

Darker took a pull on his spliff and exhaled deeply. "This wasn't what I had planned today, but I'm happy I could be there to help you. I see potential in you, Kwame. You remind me of me, which is why

Chapter 15

I wanted to help you. From here on out, we're going to have to look out for each other…you understand?"

"You saved my life," Kwame said sincerely. "I'll try and repay you any way I can."

Darker studied Kwame, his expression serious. "The police are going to come and ask you questions. They're going to scare you by telling you you're going to go to prison for what just happened. You need to understand that they're chatting shit. Me and you both know you haven't killed anyone. If they're any good at their jobs they'll know you didn't do it, too, but that's not going to stop them from trying to find out who did…and that can't happen. They won't know anything if you don't say anything, so don't say anything. Stick with 'No Comment.' Got it?"

Kwame nodded his head.

"I was actually going to bring you with us, because it's a risk leaving you behind. But maybe it's better if you're not with us if they do find us. If you promise me you'll keep your mouth shut, you can go home. Deal?" Darker stretched out his hand for a handshake.

Kwame shook his hand firmly. "Deal."

"Good. Now, get out." Said Darker.

Kwame, uncertain about where to go, got out of the car and watched as Darker also got out and walked around to the driver's side and got in. Kwame quickly went to the passenger side of the vehicle and tried to enter, but Darker locked the doors.

"No. You'll have to find your own way home. It's better that way. I need to get rid of this car. I'll call you when everything blows over." With that, Darker backed up and drove away.

Kwame looked around, trying to figure out where he was. He determined he was in Brighton. Once he found his bearings, he decided to take the train back home.

Kwame composed himself while on the train, tucking in his shirt and putting his blazer back on. When he reached his home he opened the door and rushed up the stairs. His mother shouted, "You're late!"

"Sorry, Mum. I had detention." Kwame said.

"Detention! Huh! Well, at least you're honest about it!" Julia laughed.

Kwame didn't even take off his shoes as he collapsed on his bed and went to sleep.

Chapter 16

The neighbourhood was sound asleep when the sun rose the next morning, except the usual morning joggers and other early workers. Julia had just had a shower and was making her way downstairs in her bathrobe when she noticed shadows of many individuals outside her front door. She swiftly went to the door and reached for the handle just before the armed SWAT officers booted the door inward, striking Julia and causing her to fall backward onto the floor. Six SWAT team officers holding MP5 weapons swarmed into the house. Two of the officers quickly made their way up the stairs whilst two officers secured the rooms on the main level.

Julia winced in pain as she struggled to stand. *"What are you doing in my house!"* she demanded. *"How dare you! What is this about?"*

One of the officers pushed her back onto the floor. "Shut up and put your hands where I can see them. You know why we're here, and if you don't, well then, that's worse, init?" The officer said before putting Julia's hands behind her back and placing handcuffs on, after flipping her on to her belly.

Julia screamed in pain as the officer tightened the cuffs.

"Mum!" Kwame bellowed from his room. He tried to run and help his mother but was quickly met by two large officers who were pointing

their weapons in his face. The sight of these automatic weapons made Kwame freeze as he had flashbacks to what he witnessed. He knew what a small revolver could do and imagined the power these assault weapons contained.

"Don't fucking move a muscle, kid. Don't make me have to make a mess. Put your hands up slowly." one of the officers ordered.

"Turn around," the other yelled. "Now, get on your knees." The officers then placed Kwame in handcuffs and tightened them harshly.

"You are under arrest on suspicion of murder. You do not have to say anything, but it may harm your defence if you do not mention when questioned something which you later rely on in court. Anything you do say may be given in evidence," said one of the officers as they led Kwame out of the room. Kwame could hear the policemen destroying his family's home as he walked down the stairs: glass breaking, wood being snapped, and fabrics being ripped. The police officers gripped Kwame securely as they dragged him down the stairs. Kwame looked at his mother as he was led out of the house. The tears flooding from her eyes made his water as well. As Kwame stepped outside, he was met by more officers and a crowd of nosey neighbours looking on as he was escorted into the back of the police van. Even after the doors of the van closed, he heard his mother's desperate cries. Kwame put his head against the tinted window to look at her as the vehicle took off.

At the police station, he was processed into the system for the first time. As he entered the check-in point, the officer who had so cruelly antagonised his mother whispered in Kwame's ear, "This is where the world forgets about you, boy. It's over for you, you fucking chimp."

Chapter 16

Kwame gave the officer a hateful stare as he was pushed into a processing room, where Kwame had his fingerprints and mugshot taken. He looked around at all of the officers mean-mugging him as he had his mug shots taken. Each officer was looking at him as the suspected murderer they thought he was, and if they were true, then Kwame was indeed a very dangerous individual. Kwame thought to himself how untrue this was, and how innocent he actually was. A lone tear rolled down Kwame's cheek when he was placed inside the holding cell. The cell contained only a concrete bed to lie on and smelled strongly of urine, covered by a thin plastic mattress, which also smelled of urine. The smell was so overpowering that he began to vomit out the food he had the night before in to the toilet provided in the cell, missing slightly and getting some vomit on the floor of the cell. He stumbled back as he became lightheaded and slipped on his own vomit, falling on the hard ground.

"Help!" he wailed. "Somebody help me, please!"

Moments later, an officer came and looked inside the cell. After seeing at Kwame lying on the floor in his own vomit, the officer chuckled and walked away. Kwame, now regretting his request, managed to get to the concrete bed. He had been scared before, but now became even more fearful. He'd never seen such cruelty.

He had always known that the police could be heartless, but realising he was now in the custody of people who truly did not care about his wellbeing had him panic-stricken. Lying down, he had an anxiety attack once again. He recalled his childhood when his mother taught him breathing exercises to control his anger. He closed his eyes and pictured his mother doing the breathing exercises with him, and eventually his respirations returned to normal. He kept his eyes closed and concentrated on his mother before falling asleep.

Chapter 17

The officers woke Kwame abruptly; he wasn't even sure how long he had slept. They opened the holding cell and took Kwame to an interview room, where his mother sat.

"Mum!" Kwame cried as she ran toward him and hugged him tightly. They held each other until the sound of a throat clearing alerted them to stop.

"Please be seated," said the female detective, one of two in the room. "I'm Police Constable Knight, and this is Detective McButcher."

Julia Amponsah straightened in her chair. She'd heard of this team, had read about them in the newspaper. They'd been partnered for years, working together to solve murders and other serious crimes. They were well known in the community and feared by local gangsters for their sheer tenacity to never give up.

It was said that Deborah Knight was "better than the boys." The daughter of a military officer, she'd risen through the ranks as one of the only black female detectives in her squad. She was a tall, curvy woman with long, thick black hair that was pinned into a bun. Julia noticed that her bright red lipstick matched her nails. It was her only nod to her gender; her tan blouse and brown pantsuit looked very ordinary, and she wore a stern, emotionless expression.

Detective McButcher was a retired veteran who had earned honours for bravery in the Falklands war. He joined the police force immediately after coming back from the war and had been a detective many years ago. Whilst quite old, he stood over six feet tall and appeared to be quite fit. Most of his hair was gone, but he had a thick grey moustache. He wore a black suit and the shiniest shoes Julia had ever seen.

Constable Knight addressed Kwame. "Your mother is here because you're only fourteen and we need a legal guardian present for the interview. She's adamant that you won't need any further legal counsel but it's important for you to know that a lawyer can be provided to you if you want one. Do you understand?" she said.

"My son hasn't done anything wrong," Julia declared. "He doesn't need a lawyer. How dare you!"

Kwame looked at his mother and then back at the detectives before putting his head in his hands. He thought back to the last thing Darker said to him. He knew that whatever happened, he had to keep his mouth shut. He could never snitch on the man who had saved his life.

"No, it's fine, I didn't do anything, and I don't need a lawyer."

"Okay." Constable Knight pressed the record button on the tape recorder, signalling the start of the interview."

Detective McButcher leaned toward Kwame and clasped his hands together before speaking. "My name is Detective Ian McButcher. I have with me Police Constable Deborah Knight. It's ten-thirty a.m. on the thirtieth of September, two thousand and four. I'm interviewing Kwame Amponsah, who has been charged with the triple murder that occurred yesterday—"

CHAPTER 17

Julia gasped. *"Triple murder?"* she screeched. "That's outrageous! My son is not capable of killing anyone!"

"I haven't killed anyone, Mum!" Kwame insisted. "I swear on my life, I didn't kill anyone!"

"Oh, my Lord Jesus Christ, please save us. What is going on?" Julia whimpered. "Why are you accusing my son of such a horrendous crime?"

"Kwame," Detective McButcher said in a gentle voice, "the only way we're going to know what happened, is if you *tell* us what happened. I'm just going to cut to the chase. We know you were there. We have several witnesses who saw three guys chasing after you and your friend Chris. Some of them actually called the police and reported that these guys were chasing and robbing school kids. When we found them, two of them were dead and so was your friend Chris. You, on the other hand, were nowhere to be found. What happened?"

A long silence followed as everyone in the room waited for Kwame's response. Kwame looked around the room, noticing the flashing red light on the recorder and the cameras recording him. He looked at his mother, whose palm was pressed into her chest, anxiously awaiting his answers. Then Kwame met Detective McButcher's eyes. Kwame wanted to get a sense of the man sitting across from him, wondering whether he would accept the truth for what it was. Kwame thought about how aggressively the police had carried out their warrant, even putting his innocent mother in handcuffs. If they really wanted the truth, they never would have charged him with the murders in the first place, because he didn't do it. Yet here they were, trying to crucify him.

"No comment," he finally replied.

Detective McButcher exchanged a look at Julia, then shook his head.

"If you didn't do it, Kwame," his mother pleaded, "then tell these people what they want to know! Surely you know who *did* do it. What do you mean, 'no comment'?"

Kwame simply cast his eyes downward and remained silent.

Detective McButcher continued his interrogation. "Kwame, look at me. I understand you're scared, and I understand you're wondering if we're really here to help you, but we are. I can't help you if you don't let me. I'm giving you a chance to be honest with us so that we can help you. If this was simply supposed to be a verbal altercation and something went wrong, we can understand that. If you was just defending yourself, we can understand that. I've been doing this job for years. I know what you youngsters think about snitching, but it's not true. You're entitled to tell the truth and to exonerate yourself. It all starts now, Kwame," He pleaded.

"No comment," Kwame repeated, eyes still downcast.

At that, Deborah Knight slammed her palm on the table, startling everyone in the room.

"Enough of this! We know you texted somebody to come and help you. We know that you planned this murder. We have enough evidence to proceed and go to trial. If you didn't commit the murders then tell us who did."

Kwame's heart began racing as he contemplated his options and what could possibly happen to him if he declined to cooperate. He decided to stand firm on his decision not to talk and for a third time stated, "No comment."

Chapter 17

"Your friend CJ is dead, Kwame," the detective continued. "If it wasn't you who killed him, wouldn't you want us to find the one who did and bring them to justice? By remaining silent, you're betraying your friend. You're betraying CJ," he repeated.

Kwame closed his eyes and relived the moment CJ's killer was shot dead. He chuckled under his breath before stopping himself.

"No comment," he said again.

The detectives looked at each other before shaking their heads.

Detective McButcher sighed heavily. "Interview terminated at ten thirty-five," he stated before turning off the recorder.

He and Detective Knight stood to leave. Detective McButcher paused in the doorway and looked back at Kwame.

"Well, kid, you've just ruined your life," he said sadly before leaving the room.

Kwame looked at his mother's tear-stained face as they sat in silence. An officer informed her she had to leave. She bent to give Kwame one final hug before being escorted out.

Kwame remained in the interview room alone, contemplating his fate.

Chapter 18

Kwame dozed off in the interview room, awakened by two officers he had not seen before. One of the officers ordered Kwame to stand and turn around, then placed handcuffs on him.

"What's going on?" he demanded, alarmed.

"Save your energy, lad. You've got a long day ahead of you," one of the officers replied as he escorted Kwame through the police station and out the back door, where a van awaited. The two other prisoners in the van also looked very young.

"Where are we going?" Kwame asked the officer, who simply ignored him and slammed the van door shut.

As the driver started the engine, one of the youthful offenders started laughing.

"You look like a deer in the headlights, man. I can tell you're green. We're going to Feltham. I'm being remanded, so that means you've probably been remanded, too. Stay focused." The young man spoke with an Irish accent and had a bruised face. Between the bruises and a swollen right eye, it was clear he had been beaten pretty badly. He rested his head against the window and almost instantly fell asleep as the van began making its way to the prison.

Kwame stared out of the window the whole time, taking in everything around him as he made the long hour-and-a-half journey to Feltham Prison for youthful offenders. During the journey, he thought about how he had come to be in this situation, and he began to silently cry. He thought back to the last conversation he'd had with Mr. Power, and how things could have been different if he'd just stayed inside the school. Thinking of how CJ had lost his life so senselessly made Kwame's tears flow even faster. CJ had instinctively followed him, knowing he was in trouble and trying to help, and lost his life in the process. Kwame's sadness turned to anger when he thought about Tiny Eyez and how he'd started all this. Tiny Eyez should have been the one to die, but he was still alive while CJ was dead, Kwame thought to himself. Then and there, Kwame vowed that he would avenge CJ's death by finding Tiny Eyez and killing him, no matter how long it took.

At that moment, all fear left Kwame's spirit. His pounding heartbeat began to slow to normal. He was a man on a mission, and nothing would stop him from completing it.

After a long drive on the motorway, they finally reached the prison and were taken inside to begin processing into the system. Kwame instantly noticed that the prison was extremely secure, with really high walls and barbed wiring around the property. Once inside, Kwame immediately felt claustrophobic by the bars that separated each sector. The second youth from the van began crying as the door closed behind them. The young Irishman who had spoken to Kwame earlier laughed.

"You're all fucked, man!" he said between his laughter. Turning to a prison officer, he said, "Can you fucking hurry up, please? I'm fucking knackered! I'll sleep well tonight, I'll tell you that!"

Chapter 18

Kwame and the other youth offenders were ushered to a waiting room, whilst each new prisoner was strip searched and given their new prison reference and prison garb. Kwame stood with his back to the wall of the large cell he was assigned to with five other inmates.

Matthew Knightley, the Governor of the Young Offender's prison, had taken time out of his busy schedule to conduct the prisoners' induction. Matthew banged on the window violently, alerting those who were heavy into their sleep waiting to be called. Matthew pointed at Kwame and waved for him to come through.

Kwame looked at each of the remaining young men in the holding cell, nodding at each of them as a way of showing respect before leaving the holding cell. He walked through to where he was instructed by Mr. Knightley.

"I need you to take all of your clothes off and place them in this bag. You'll get these back when you're released." Said Matthew.

Kwame looked at Matthew who had his eyes fixated on Kwame.

"Are you a paedophile or something? Are you not going to turn around?" Said Kwame

Matthew laughed and shook his head. "You belong to me now," he said, "You don't get any privacy here sunshine. Now strip."

Kwame removed his clothes and put them in the bag. Matthew then instructed him to bend over and cough. After doing this, Kwame was given his new prison clothes and plimsole shoes. After Kwame put these on, he was escorted through to his new home.

The murders of three youths on the street in broad daylight had made national news, and Kwame was considered a high-profile prisoner. For this reason, he was brought to one of the most secure wings of the prison. The G wing held Britain's most vicious and troubled youths. All prison officers entering that wing had to first don additional riot gear due to the volatile nature of the prisoners.

Panic grew in Kwame's gut when he saw the extra protective gear the guards of the wing wore. As soon as the heavy metal door opened, Kwame heard chaos and shouting. He froze and had to be dragged down the hall. As he passed cell after cell, the young men commented on his arrival.

"Fresh meat!" one of the prisoners yelled with excitement. "Yeah, he looks like a bitch!" shouted another before laughing hysterically.

Kwame was led to a cell on the upper deck of the wing, where he was met by his new cellmate.

"Enjoy your new home," said the guard before pushing Kwame into the small cell and locking it.

Kwame stood just inside the cell, locking eyes with his new cellmate. The young man slid off the top bunk and stood, and Kwame estimated his height at six-foot-three. As he stood with his arms folded and a stern expression on his face, Kwame observed the multiple scars on his face and arms. He then looked around at the rest of the cell, noticing the toilet, sink, and the toiletries surrounding it. He noticed the huge stock of food and other household items.

"You can look if you want," the teenager said in a tone neither friendly nor menacing. "But if you ever lay a finger on my shit, I'll cut off both your hands, big man."

"I ain't gonna touch your stuff as long as you don't touch mine. You leave me alone and I'll leave you alone. If we're going to live

CHAPTER 18

together, we might as well look out for each other, too. I'm Kwame. What's good, bro?" Kwame extended his fist to greet his new cellmate.

The man gave him a reluctant stare before tapping Kwame's fist with his own.

"My name is Jason, but the roads call me Rager." The introduction seemed to lighten the tension.

"Top bunk is mine." Rager said, before jumping back on his bed to reinitiate his sleep.

As Rager relaxed on his bed and tried to go back to sleep, and Kwame began setting up his bed, he was confronted by other prisoners on the wing. Four prisoners had swarmed his cell. One of the prisoners grabbed Kwame by the neck and pinned him to the wall in his cell.

"Word on the street is you're here for murder big man! Is that true?" Said the prisoner.

Kwame tried to remain calm as the prisoner continued to choke him.

"Are you Younger Darker?" Said the prisoner. Kwame looked at the other prisoners who had infiltrated his cell. He then looked over at his cellmate, who was mouthing the words "Don't have it, fight back!"

Kwame then immediately proceeded to overpower the prisoner. Kwame headbutted the assailant, and quickly executed a barrage of punches, breaking the prisoner's nose.

"Ahh, fuck man!" Said the prisoner, "I was only playing with you ak!" The prisoner spat out the blood in his mouth on Kwame's cell floor. Kwame looked at the inmate who assaulted him, and then glared at the other prisoners in his cell.

"GET THE FUCK OUT OF MY CELL UNLESS YOU'RE TRYING TO FIGHT ME RIGHT NOW!" Screamed Kwame. Startled and shocked, the prisoners exited the cell. Shortly after, all inmates on the wing were locked down for the rest of the day.

"YESS!" Said Jason, "That's how you're supposed to handle shit! Nobody is gonna take you for an idiot again! You might have made some enemies, but I would rather have identifiable enemies than have everybody in here think they can violate me. Feel me?"

"Yeah, I hear you." Replied Kwame.

As Kwame began cleaning the blood and other debris in the cell, he began to panic about what was coming next. He had just had a fight with people he didn't know on the first day. He also didn't know how long he would be there. After cleaning his cell, he decided that sleeping was the only way to get rid of the nervous feelings he was having. Kwame got in bed and tried to sleep straight away, but couldn't get comfortable on the hard concrete base, covered by the thinnest of mattresses. After thirty minutes of twisting and turning as he tried to find the best position, he finally fell asleep.

Chapter 19

Kwame was awakened the next day by the sounds of his roommate exercising. He rubbed his eyes and stretched as he sat up in bed.

"Good morning, my bro." Jason greeted between push-ups. "Come, join me in a workout. You'll feel better!"

Kwame got up, brushed his teeth and washed his face at the sink before joining Jason in his exercise routine. They did one hundred push-ups each and then did one hundred sit-ups. After that, they both did three sets of squats before collapsing on their beds. The doors opened a few hours later, and Kwame and Jason began preparing to make their way to the showers.

Before they walked down the cellblock, Jason sternly said to Kwame, "Hear what I'm saying. When we leave this cell, we're gonna cut through quickly, shower together, and leave. Quick ones."

Kwame gave him an incredulous stare. "Fam, are you gay? You must be skunked if you think I'm going to shower with you! I don't swing that way! You can shower first and I'll go after!"

Jason slapped his forehead. "You just got attacked last night and now you're accusing your cellmate of being a battyman? You must have a death wish! Do you?"

"No." Kwame replied.

"Well, if you want to live, then follow my instructions. If you weren't my cellmate, I wouldn't care what happened to you. But I've been here three years now and I've never had an issue. I don't need you bringing me drama because you're not moving on point," Jason hissed. "Now, follow me."

Jason and Kwame entered the bathroom at the end of the hall. From the moment Kwame left his cell, he noticed everyone standing and staring at the two of them. Fear took hold, and he tried to hide it, but he expected a continuation of the violence that had ensued yesterday.

Kwame and Jason reached the showers and exhaled with relief upon realising they were alone.

"Listen, I'll stand guard," Jason said, "so hurry up and shower. They could be coming in here any minute."

Kwame rapidly removed his clothes and jumped into the shower. He flinched and quickly jumped out as the ice-cold water hit his body through the broken showerhead. "Fuck, that's cold!"

"And it's not going to get warmer, so hurry up!" Jason ordered.

Kwame braced himself before stepping back into the freezing cold shower. He washed and rinsed in record time. After drying off, he stood guard as Jason showered just as quickly. Then they made their way back to their cell. On the way back, the other prisoners continued to give them deathly stares.

When Kwame returned to his cell, he immediately noticed two designer tracksuits folded neatly on his bunk, along with two pairs

Chapter 19

of Nike trainers. A note lay on top of the suit. Kwame picked it up and read it.

> *"Thanks for standing tall and keeping your mouth shut. You've proved you're a real one and gained my respect. I promise you as long as you stick by the code, my guys will take care of you whilst you're in the wokhouse, and as long as you keep your mouth shut, you'll buss case. They know you didn't do anything, they just know you know something. The only way you're going to stay in jail is if you snitch on yourself. Remember that. See you soon my young G. Stay up and stay safe. - Darker".*

A broad grin spread over Kwame's face as he took a closer look at his new clothes. One of the tracksuits had a Nike label, its black-and-white colours matching one pair of the gym shoes. The other tracksuit was by Louis Vuitton, which Kwame knew was worth thousands of pounds. If this was his reward for loyalty, he would continue to show allegiance. Nobody had ever bought him anything so valuable.

Jason picked up one of Kwame's new trainers and sniffed the inside of it before exhaling with pleasure. "Ahh, that smells so good! These are brand new, fam! I haven't smelled this in ages! You're lucky you got small feet, otherwise I'd take these from you!"

"Yeah, and you would have died trying, big man!" Kwame replied.

Jason chuckled and put down the shoe. "I would have said you're chatting shit if you didn't have murder on your charges!"

Chapter 20

Kwame put on his new Nike tracksuit and trainers before going back out onto the landing. He wanted to know who dropped him the new clothing. He looked around at the other prisoners who were out of their cells at the time. Some were talking with other prisoners on the landing, others were making their way to the showers or engaging in leisurely activities. As Kwame continued scanning the landing he locked eyes with the prisoner who had entered his cell the day before, asking him if he was Younger Darker. Kwame got the impression that the prisoner was waiting to be acknowledged, so he nodded at the man, who returned the greeting and signalled for him to come to his cell.

Kwame and Jason sat on their beds as the prisoner entered their cell with seeming reluctance.

"Was this you?" asked Kwame, tugging on the jacket of his tracksuit. At the prisoner's nod, Kwame asked, "What's your name?"

"My name is Jerome, but the mandem call me M-face. Darker is the OG. He told us to make sure you were looked after when you came on the wing. Darker doesn't recruit wastemen, let alone make people his younger, so you must be certified," M-face explained. "The other dons who came with me yesterday are part of the team as well.

You're going to have to apologise for moving mad when I introduce you properly. If you ever need anything, just holla at us, init. Respect."

M-face put out his fist in a parting gesture. After a momentary hesitation, Kwame tapped his fist against Jerome's. He then turned and left the cell.

Kwame exchanged glances with Jason, who had sat on his bunk watching the exchange with Jerome. Jason merely shrugged before lying down.

Hours later, the cell doors opened once again for recreational time. This was Kwame's first opportunity to take in the fresh air since he reached the prison. He put on his new clothes and trainers and made his way to the yard. As Kwame entered the recreational garden at the rear of the prison, he took several deep breaths. The fresh air smelled sweet compared to the stale fumes that circulated within the prison walls.

Kwame's eyes took it in, trying to familiarise himself with his surroundings. He noticed that the majority of the inmates stood in groups and that the groups seemed to be segregated by colour. He spotted M-face standing in a group. M-face caught his eye and waved to Kwame to join him.

An eerie silence occurred as Kwame passed each group on his way over to M-face. The other inmates had stopped their conversations to observe this fish make his way through a sea of sharks. Kwame was careful not to lock eyes with any of the inmates who were staring. He didn't have to worry about touching anyone; they backed out of his way as he passed.

Although the prison entrance was only about ten yards from where Jerome and the others stood, to Kwame it looked like miles.

Chapter 20

Instinct told him that Jerome and his crew were up to no good. Kwame felt an overwhelming feeling of hopelessness come over him. Air completely left his lungs. It was all he could do not to pass out as he greeted Jerome.

Don't show any weakness, Kwame instructed himself, breathing deeply. *Game face.* He looked at the four other young men surrounding Jerome, standing at the ready. One was growling like a guard dog that senses danger. Another kept eye contact with Kwame, not blinking once as his fist closed around something out of sight under his jacket. *What are they going to do?*

"What's going on?" he asked in a low, cautious tone.

"Listen, we don't have long. The screws are supposed to give us one hour rec time every day. But they only give us thirty minutes each time. Fucking pigs." M-face said to Kwame. "But listen, I spoke to Darker before you even got here, my bro. You know the clothes are from him. Give us your details, and we'll put money on your books, too. As long as you keep it G, it's all love. Right now, you've just got one job, you know what that is, init?"

"No. What is it?" Kwame replied.

"Do you have a trial date?"

"Yes, next week."

Jerome lowered his chin to his chest. "Next week! Raah, they must really be onto you! I've been in here two months, and I don't even have a trial date. But listen, your job is simple, ak. Don't tell them anything. Do you understand? Darker saved your life, and you need to return the favour. *That's* your job, and it's an easy one. Don't fuck up, you understand? If you do, then, your family…"

Kwame contemplated the implications of Jerome's words. M-face had a point. Darker *had* saved his life. Had it not been for his intervention, Kwame would have been dead in the street.

"Yes, Darker saved my life," he said. "I don't even know the name of the girl who pulled the trigger, so I ain't gonna say shit."

Jerome carefully studied Kwame's eyes, as if he could find the truth through Kwame's pupils. He placed his arm on Kwame's shoulder and gripped it firmly. "It's easy to talk that talk now, my guy, but if the feds don't have any proper evidence, then they're going to blame you. This is your first charge, so don't panic and start talking shit when they start telling you you're going to spend the rest of your life in prison. I promise you, the best thing you can do is say nothing. It's not gonna be easy, so you need to stay strong."

Kwame took a deep breath. "Yeah, I hear you." You don't need to worry about me. Trust me. I won't let you down."

After a few moments of awkward silence, Jerome broke the tension with a hearty laugh. "I like you man! You're the real deal, init!" He chuckled. He turned to the others in the group. "Listen, this young rottweiler is Tiny Spar. That growling shit ain't a joke. He's really on stuff! The tall nigga is Younger Lighter, and that's Younger Inches."

Kwame spudded each one and instantly felt much more relaxed. They spent the rest of their time cracking jokes and rapping to each other before they were ordered back to their cells.

Chapter 21

After a few months had passed, Kwame had settled into his routine within the prison walls. After receiving a letter that his trial date had been pushed back, similar to the other prisoners, his anxiety about his upcoming court appearance lessened, and he spent his days going to education. It provided the mental stimulation he needed to cope with the monotonous nature of prison life. The classroom was similar to the one he'd known at his secondary school, students spent their time making jokes, laughing, and conversing with friends. The teacher was a mature woman called Regina Mugabe, who was definitely the highlight of the youthful offenders' day. She was a tall, voluptuous woman from Guyana in her late thirties, who always wore a satin black shirt, with a grey skirt which hugged her body but covered her ankles, along with bright red heels, with lipstick to match. She was a fierce, strict teacher who didn't take any lip from the youth offenders. To many of the young men, she provided them with a motherly figure they never had before, and they respected her immensely.

"Good morning, Miss Mugabe," Kwame said as he entered the classroom. How good she smelled, he thought, compared to the stench that floated through the prison. Her perfume was heavenly.

"Good morning, son!" she replied. "I hope you read the book I gave you. I know it will help you."

"It did. I really related to the shepherd's journey in that book. It made me realise that everything happens for a reason."

"Good!" Miss Mugabe pressed her palms together. "I'm happy you understood the message. Everything happens for a reason, and your journey doesn't end within these walls. Now take a seat. We will begin shortly."

Kwame took a seat in the rear of the classroom next to Jerome, who had become his close friend. Jerome was also the only person within his social circle who shared his thirst for knowledge.

"Fam, you need to stop moving to my wife before I wet you up!" Jerome said in a mock stern manner.

They looked at each other through narrowed eyes for a few seconds in silence before bursting out in laughter.

"It's not my fault you're too shook to speak to her! But if it's like that, I can let her know on your behalf, init. Just say the word," Kwame said with a shrug.

"Nah, trust me, I talk with my eyes. She'll come to me eventually." Jerome chuckled.

Kwame joined in as he prepared for the mathematics class.

"You've got court tomorrow finally, init?" Jerome asked.

"Yeah, man. Judgement day."

"I hear you, bro. I hope everything goes your way. We need real niggas like you helping Darker hold shit down on the outside. Like

Chapter 21

I said, don't say shit and you'll buss case, trust me." Jerome bumped fists with Kwame.

Everyone was now seated, and Miss Mugabe began the lesson.

"Today we're going to learn how to add two fractions," she began. "First, you have to understand what a fraction is. A fraction is part of a whole, such as a half, a quarter, an eighth …."

Jerome and Kwame continued talking in the back of the room.

Kwame and Jerome abruptly halted their conversation, looking forward in time to see the teacher standing just a few feet away from them.

"I do not appreciate you choosing to talk in my class. You come here to learn. If you don't want to learn, then you need to leave. You're disturbing the other students."

"I'm sorry, Miss. I'm listening," Kwame apologised, promptly opening his notebook and picking up a pencil. Jerome, on the other hand, kept his notebook closed and sat sulking with his arms crossed, which elicited chuckles and snorts from the others in the room.

"You heard what I said, Jerome," Miss Mugabe continued, "If you don't want to learn, leave. You're not going to sit here and disrupt my class."

"Fuck it, then!" Jerome boomed, picking up his books and standing. "I'm out." He turned to Kwame. "You coming?"

He didn't hesitate. "Nah, I'm gonna stay. My mum wants me to pass my GCSEs while I'm here. Gotta learn this stuff if that's gonna happen. I'll check you later, though?" he added, his voice hopeful.

"Say nothing. I'm out, man. I ain't got time for you nerds." Jerome huffed as he headed out the door. Some of the Caucasian boys in the class immediately began singing the "na na na na" chorus from the popular chant, "Na Na Na Na, Wa-aaa-ve, Goodbye." It wasn't often that they could get away with ridiculing M-face, who was widely feared on the wing.

A ginger-haired, freckled youth called Ron stood up and took a final jab.

"Fuck me! Who walks away from spending time out of their cell just because they can't shut up for a few hours! Christ! You really are a lost cause, init? No wonder nobody on the outside comes to visit you! Even they know you're a lost cause!"

Jerome halted just inches from the door. The room fell silent, as the youths surrounding Ron went pale. They knew that Ron had made a big mistake pushing past the boundary of disrespect. Kwame also tensed, awaiting Jerome's response. Ron looked at his peers, who were shaking their heads at him. An almost palpable mood shift occurred, darkness descending on the room.

The silence was broken by Jerome's maniacal cackle.

"I was just playing, M-face," Ron said nervously. "I'm sorry man."

Jerome, his back still to them, just kept laughing.

"All right, Jerome. He apologized to you. Would you please go, now?" Miss Mugabe urged.

Jerome suddenly stopped laughing and turned to stare at Ron. "Nah, that was funny!" Jerome said, slowly moving toward him. Ron's friends quickly stood and surrounded him in a human shield.

Chapter 21

Jerome squinted in genuine confusion. "We're good, man. You lot don't need to do all that. I just wanna spud my man before I leave. It took balls to talk to me like that. I didn't expect it." He held out his fist. Ron nervously stepped through the human shield to offer his fist in an act of making peace. Their fists connected.

"I proper rate you still! You called me a lost cause, and you know what?" Jerome said.

"What?" Ron's voice sounded unnaturally high-pitched.

Their hands lowered. Jerome leaned forward and said in a stage whisper, "You're absolutely right. The devil took me years ago."

Jerome's smile didn't fool Kwame for a moment. He had never seen Jerome smile like that, like the Joker in the Batman comics he had in his cell. Ron looked uneasy as well as he backed away. Then, within a split second, Jerome snatched his sharpened pencil from his pocket and stabbed Ron in the neck. Blood flew out of Ron's neck with intense force, like water coming from a hose. Miss Mugabe screamed and ran to the door to call for help as Jerome stabbed Ron until the pencil snapped inside his neck.

Three prison guards rushed in. Two of them restrained M-face, while the third knelt beside Ron and tried to stem the bleeding with one hand while radioing for medical assistance with the other. Jerome laughed as the guards escorted him out of the classroom. He shouted to Kwame over his shoulder,

"Remember what I told you, Kwame. Don't say shit tomorrow, and you won't end up like that cunt on the floor!" Then he cackled maniacally, the sound still audible as the door closed behind him.

As Jerome's laughing became more distant, Kwame watched the guard and Miss Mugabe try to stem Ron's bleeding. Blood had spurted everywhere, and Ron was gagging and choking. Kwame was trembling, and the entire room seemed paralysed with fear. No one said a word until after Ron was carried out on a stretcher, and Miss Mugabe had dismissed them.

Chapter 22

The next morning, the screws came to collect Kwame from his cell to transport him to court. As they unlocked the cell door, Kwame closed his eyes and said a brief prayer.

"Good luck, my broski," Jason said as Kwame left.

"Thanks," he replied.

It took another hour for Kwame to be processed out of the prison. He was escorted outside, where a van similar to the one that had brought him here awaited. Its windows were tinted black, and on the inside was a cage within a cage. Kwame was cuffed to the bench he sat on before the van began to move. Even though no one could see inside the van, Kwame was able to see out of it.

He'd forgotten how much he enjoyed just witnessing life. His eyes took everything in… schoolchildren getting on the big red bus, billboards advertising products he wasn't allowed to possess within his small, confined cell, his favourite restaurants: McDonald's, KFC, Cream's, and Morley's. Every time he passed one, his belly grumbled with hunger and he could practically taste his favourite meals. At that moment, Kwame concluded that taking away one's freedom was indeed the most severe punishment known to man.

The drive to the courthouse took approximately ninety minutes. Due to the notoriety of his case, Kwame had found himself standing trial at the famous Old Bailey. Upon arrival, he saw that the media was already waiting for him. A mob of them ran up to the van and snapped photos, although they were not able to see Kwame sitting inside.

"Looks like you're a celebrity!" chuckled the transport officer, "Make sure you give a big smile for the cameras!" The officers laughed among themselves before opening the van doors, exposing Kwame to the horde of reporters. As Kwame was escorted inside, he was bombarded with questions and exclamations from media people and spectators alike. Some spectators were screaming, "Murderer!" while reporters were asking, "Why did you do it, Kwame?" Through the chaos, Kwame heard someone who sounded familiar calling his name. All the faces were a blur, so he tried to drown out the other voices and focus on the one calling his name. He couldn't determine where it was coming from before he was rushed through the courthouse doors.

Kwame was led to a back room, where he met his duty solicitor. The solicitor was a young, freckled man with fiery ginger hair, with a rough ginger beard to match. He wore a rumpled grey suit with a bright blue tie and worn-looking loafers. Kwame sat in silence for a few minutes as he watched his solicitor read through several documents. Finally, the duty solicitor sighed heavily with exasperation before looking at Kwame and folding his arms.

"My name is Mr. McGinn as you know already, we met a few weeks ago. I'm the duty solicitor who's been assigned to your case. Daria, your previous duty solicitor, is no longer able to take on this case due to having to take emergency leave, so it was turned

Chapter 22

over to me. It's obvious you didn't commit this crime. Based on the conversation we had before, I personally do not think you're capable of this kind of violence. I also find it hard to believe that you went to school with a loaded firearm without anybody noticing. The issue here, though, is that the CCTV footage outside of your school shows you being chased by the deceased victims. The prosecution will argue that you committed these crimes in self-defence, which won't help you even if it was the truth." He hesitated before continuing. "There's also some more bad news. One of the witnesses at the scene has signed a statement claiming he saw you shoot and kill his two friends. However, I'm unsure if the prosecution will use this because his account of what happened doesn't match the forensic evidence from the scene."

"In other words, he's lying," Kwame said.

"Yes, but the prosecution is running with it in order to bolster their case against you. If they do try and present it to the jury, it'll be easy to dismantle it, so not to worry, hopefully. Fingers crossed. Now, with all that being said, you're the one who knows exactly what happened, and for you to remain quiet all this time, means you're either scared of the person who *did* do the murders, or you feel you can't tell on them because by killing the ones who were after you, they saved your life. Well, I'm telling you now, you need to tell the truth about what happened, or you're going to go to prison for a very long time. Do you understand?"

"Yeah, I understand," Kwame replied.

The solicitor stared at Kwame for a long moment. "So, what are you going to do?"

"I'm not going to do anything. I didn't kill anybody. It's your job to help me prove that in court. They're not going to believe me anyway. Just do your job."

Mr. McGinn sighed heavily once more before standing up, shaking Kwame's hand, and leaving the room.

Another hour or so went by before Kwame was escorted into the courtroom. As he entered, he saw his parents and Natasha sitting in the front row. Kwame smiled and waved. He realized it had been Natasha's voice he'd heard calling his name out in the crowd. Seeing her there filled him with joy, and he smiled from ear to ear.

There didn't appear to be an empty seat in the courtroom. Kwame, along with everyone else, stood when the judge entered and took his seat. As Kwame looked around at the white wigs and black gowns, including the ones worn by his own solicitor, the reality began to sink in even more that his life was on the line.

The moment the session officially began, Kwame began zoning out, and the rest of the day passed in a blur. From the opening statements to the presentation of evidence, everything seemed to move in a fast-forwarded fashion. The only time Kwame paid close attention was when CCTV footage of that fateful day was shown. Kwame relived CJ's last moments as he saw himself running away from his school gates. The camera picked up on the three men chasing after him and CJ, along with the large zombie killer blades that they were wielding.

"I know it's tough to watch, but this helps your case, Kwame," Mr. McGinn whispered. "Trust me."

Kwame nodded in acknowledgement before glancing at his mother and Natasha, his shoulders jerking at the at the horror

Chapter 22

on their faces as they watched. He scanned the crowded room for more familiar faces and saw Darker and Sweets sitting at the back of the courtroom. Kwame's heart skipped a beat as they smiled and acknowledged him from across the room. Darker placed his finger on his lip and mouthed "Shhh.." as Sweets giggled to herself as he did so. At that very moment, Kwame wanted to scream out, "The murderer is right there!" but he simply could not do it. Instead, he nodded his head to show Darker that he understood. Seeing this, his mother turned around to try and see who Kwame was interacting with, but with no luck.

It took another two weeks for all the evidence to be presented to the jury. Kwame enjoyed the trips to and from the court as he was able to observe life on the outside of the prison. On the final day of deliberations, the judge gave his instruction to the jury.

"You have been given the great burden of proving without any reasonable doubt, that the defendant is guilty or not guilty for the crimes that have called us here today. We ask that you give this your utmost attention and honesty when making your decision, which must be unanimous," said the judge, before leaving the court.

Kwame blew a kiss to his mother before being escorted out to head back to the prison. For the rest of the day, Kwame pondered on how the day had gone. He spent hours relaying the events to Jason.

"I wonder if Darker was there to show me support, or whether he just wanted to make sure I didn't snitch," Kwame pondered. "He hasn't reached out to me once since I've been here other than the note and the clothes when I arrived, and suddenly he shows up in court. At least he knows I didn't snitch on him."

"Don't take it personally that your older hasn't hollered at you." Replied Jason, "He probably knows that the jakes are monitoring your communications, and he doesn't want to bait shit out. But don't worry, my young G. You've done everything by the code. I admire you, standing tall. Not everybody has the heart to do that. And from what you've said, it looks like you might buss case as well! When you come out, your name's gonna ring out. It already is. Just be careful. Nobody wants to be a popular name amongst the demons."

Chapter 23

Three days passed as Kwame awaited his fateful verdict. During that time, Kwame experienced the same recurring dream. In the dream, he was visited by a beautiful black woman with long brown dreadlocks that stretched all the way down to her feet. She wore a creamy satin dress with a gold bow around the waist, with large wings protruding from her back. In Kwame's dream, the angel constantly told him that God was with him and that even though things were about to get much worse for him, his true father was coming to save him. The angel then flew off before he could ask what that meant.

Kwame thought about the outside world and all the things he wanted to accomplish in his life. He daydreamed about having a family with Natasha, and a well-paid job that allowed him to purchase his favourite sports car. He was enjoying that daydream for the umpteenth time when a prison guard came and stood outside his cell.

"Looks like you've got court tomorrow, son. You'll leave right after breakfast," the guard said.

Kwame nodded. "Thanks, Benny. You're a good person. I appreciate you not being a prick."

Benny chuckled. "Well, I appreciate *you* for not giving me a reason to be one." With that, he disappeared down the cellblock.

The next morning, Kwame found himself in the courthouse once again. He met his mother's gaze and tried to give her a reassuring smile. After everyone was seated, the room fell silent as it was time for the verdict to be read.

"On count one, the defendant has been charged with murder in the first degree. The jury has reached a unanimous verdict for this charge." The judge paused and took a deep breath before looking at Kwame directly.

"The jury finds Kwame Amponsah guilty on count one," she proclaimed.

Kwame's mother let out a strangled cry. She hugged herself and rocked back and forth as the judge read the remainder of the verdict.

Kwame had been found guilty of all charges brought against him.

Kwame felt lightheaded, and in his shock all of his senses began to fail him. His vision became blurry, his hearing lessened, his nose became blocked, and all moisture left his mouth. "How could this have happened?" he said softly in bewilderment. "What the fuck?"

"What the fuck?" he yelled, the enormity of what had just happened settling over him.

The judge banged her gavel vigorously as she ordered for Kwame's mother to be removed from the courtroom.

"I appreciate the nature of the news isn't what Mrs. Amponsah was looking for, but we are not done, and the courtroom must be respected."

Chapter 23

Kwame began to cry as he helplessly watched three large security officers' man-handle his mother, dragging her out of the courtroom.

"Now…" the judge continued, "this case has been quite peculiar indeed. As I look at this young boy standing in front of me, I do not believe he is capable of shooting two people in the head. I am even less convinced that Kwame is responsible for the stabbing death of his self-proclaimed best friend. I do believe that there is a large part of this story missing here, and ultimately, it is your willingness to hide this part of the story that has landed you with this verdict. You were there. The DNA tells us this. If you truly did not do this, you know who did. I hope that one day, you tell us the full truth, for your own good, but also for the peace of mind of the victims' families. Based on the unanimous decision of the jury, that has found you guilty on three counts of murder. I sentence you to life in prison, to serve a minimum of twenty-five years."

The judge banged her gavel one more time, sealing Kwame's fate.

End of Part 1